CHRISTMAS WITH THE SINGLE DAD

BY
LOUISA HEATON

MILLS
BOON®
™

First published in Great Britain 2016
By Mills & Boon, an imprint of HarperCollins*Publishers*
1 London Bridge Street, London, SE1 9GF

Large Print edition 2017

© 2016 Louisa Heaton

ISBN: 978-0-263-06706-4

'Well…maybe I'll see you later, then?'

He nodded. 'Yes. Goodbye, Sydney.'

And then, with some hesitation, Nathan leaned in and kissed the side of her face.

She sucked in a breath. His lips had only brushed her cheek, and had been gone again before she could truly appreciate it, but for the millisecond he'd made contact her body had almost imploded. Her heart had threatened to jump out of her chest. Her face must have looked as red as a stop sign.

She watched him turn and walk across the road to his place of work and stood there, breathing heavily, her fingers pressed to her face where his lips had been, and wondered what on earth she was doing.

With this *friendship* with Dr Nathan Jones.

Dear Reader,

Parenthood is not an easy thing. None of us is really experienced when we go home with that newborn baby in our arms, no matter how many nieces, nephews, cousins or younger siblings we might have cared for. Looking after your *own* child is completely different, and we can only hope we'll muddle through and know what we're doing.

Sydney Harper, my veterinary surgeon heroine, is a mother *without* a child, desperately trying to get through the days, and my hero doctor, Nathan Jones, is having to be both mother *and* father to his daughter, whilst fighting the knowledge that he has a medical condition that could possibly make their lives even harder.

Being a parent with a chronic medical condition is hard. I know this from personal experience. But the reserves of strength you draw on, knowing that you have to get through each day for the sake of your children, is as strong as your intense love for them, and you'll do anything not to let them down. We see this in Nathan, and it's the kind of strength that Sydney needs in her life. She is pulled to Nathan like a moth to a sea of flame.

I hope you'll enjoy their story, and that if you have children you'll give them an extra-big hug before they go to sleep.

Happy reading!

Louisa xxx

Louisa Heaton lives on Hayling Island, Hampshire, with her husband, four children and a small zoo. She has worked in various roles in the health industry—most recently four years as a Community First Responder, answering 999 calls. When not writing, Louisa enjoys other creative pursuits, including reading, quilting and patchwork—usually instead of the things she *ought* to be doing!

Books by Louisa Heaton

Mills & Boon Medical Romance

The Baby That Changed Her Life
His Perfect Bride?
A Father This Christmas?
One Life-Changing Night
Seven Nights with Her Ex

Visit the Author Profile page
at millsandboon.co.uk for more titles.

For Mrs Duff, my first English teacher,
for telling me I had a wonderful imagination
and that I was never to stop writing.

CHAPTER ONE

SYDNEY HARPER CONFIRMED her appointment details on the surgery's check-in touchscreen and headed into the waiting room.

It was full. Much too full. Eleven of the twelve available chairs were filled with faces she recognised. People she saw every day in the village. One or two of her own clients from the veterinary practice she ran. Were they *all* before her? Would she be sitting in this waiting room all morning to see Dr Preston? She had patients of her own waiting—it was a busy time of year. Close to Christmas. No doubt everyone was trying to see their doctor before the festive season.

With a sigh at the thought of the inevitable wait she strode in, looking for the book she always kept in her bag for situations such as this.

At the empty seat she sat down and opened the book, slipping her bookmark into her fingers.

She tried to focus on the words upon the page, but her eyes were tired and she kept reading the same sentence over and over again. The words were refusing to go in and make sense.

It was happening again. Every year when it started to get close to *that date* her body rebelled and she couldn't sleep. The date would be hanging heavy in the near future, along with the dread of having to get through Christmas again, reliving what had happened before, every moment as clear as if it had just occurred. The shock. The fear. The *guilt*.

The difficulty getting to sleep. Then the difficulty *staying* asleep. She'd keep waking, staring at the clock, staring at those bright red digits, watching them tick over, minute to minute, hour to hour. Feeling *alone*. So alone in the dark! With no one to talk to. No one to go to, to reassure herself that everyone was fine.

That first year—the first anniversary of when it had happened—she'd got up and stood in the doorway of Olivia's old room, staring at her daughter's empty bed. She'd stood there almost all night. Trying to remember what it had looked like when it had been filled with life and laughter and joy.

The second year after it had happened she'd got up again and, determined not to stand in the doorway for another night, gawking at nothing, she'd decided to make herself useful. She'd cleaned. Scrubbing the oven in the middle of the night until it shone like a new pin was perfect therapy as far as she was concerned. She could get angry with the burnt-on bits. Curse at them. Moan about the ache in her back from all the bending over. But it felt better to be focused on a real physical pain than a mental one.

Last year, when the anniversary of Olivia's death had come around, she'd decided to visit Dr Preston and he'd given her a prescription for some sleeping pills and told her to come and see him if it happened again.

This year, though her oven could no doubt do with another clean, the idea of being up all night again—alone again—just wasn't an option. She hated losing all this sleep. And it wasn't just the one night any more. She was losing sleep earlier and earlier, up to a month or more before the anniversary.

So here she was.

All she needed was a quick prescription. She could be in and out in seconds. Get back to her own patients—Fletcher the Great Dane, who needed his paw checked after a grass seed had become embedded under his pad, a health check on two new ferrets and the first set of jabs for Sara's new kitten. There were others, she knew, but they were her first three and they would be waiting. Even now. Patiently watching the clock in *her* waiting room.

The screen on the wall in front of her gave a beep and she looked up to see if she was being called in. It wasn't, but the person next to her got up out of her chair and left. Sydney was glad for the space, but it didn't last long, Mrs Courtauld, owner of a retired greyhound, settled into the newly vacant seat.

'Hello, Sydney. How nice to see you. How are you doing?'

'Mrs C! I'm fine. How are you?'

'Oh, you know. The usual aches and pains.

That's why I'm here. My knees are giving me a bit of gyp. They have been ever since Prince knocked me over in the park and broke my wrist.'

'You did get quite a knock, didn't you?'

'I did! But at my age you expect a bit of wear and tear in the old joints. I'm no spring chicken now, you know. I get out and about each day if I can. It's good to keep mobile.'

Sydney nodded, smiling. 'But you're still looking great, Mrs C.'

'You're too kind, young Sydney. I do have mirrors in the house—I know how old I look. The skin on my neck is that red and saggy I'm amazed a farmer hasn't shot me, thinking I'm an escaped turkey.'

Sydney laughed. 'Ridiculous! I'd be happy to look like you if I ever make it to pensionable age.'

Mrs Courtauld snorted. 'Of course you'll make it to my age! What are you now? Thirty-three? Thirty-four?'

'Thirty-five.'

'You see? Loads of years left in you.' She thought for a moment, her eyes darkening, and she looked hard at Sydney in concern. 'Unless, of course, you're here because there's something wrong? Oh, Sydney, you're not dreadfully ill, are you?'

Mrs Courtauld's face filled with motherly concern and she laid a liver-spotted wrinkly hand on Sydney's arm.

'Just not sleeping very well.'

Mrs Courtauld nodded, looking serious. 'No. 'Course not. The anniversary is coming up again, isn't it? Little Olivia?'

Sydney swallowed hard, touched that Mrs Courtauld had realised the date was near. How many in the village had forgotten? *Don't cry.*

'Yes. It is,' she answered, her voice low. She wasn't keen on anyone else in the waiting room listening in.

Mrs Courtauld gripped Sydney's hand and squeezed it. 'Of course. Understandable. I'm the same each year when it comes round to my Alfred's birthday. Ten years since I lost him.' She paused as she looked off, as if into the distance. But then she perked up again. 'I laid some flowers at Alfred's grave the other day and I thought of you. Your little Olivia's plot is so close. I hope you don't mind, but I put an amaryllis against her headstone.'

Oh.

Sydney wasn't sure how to respond. That was sweet. It was nice to think that Olivia had a bright, beautiful flower to brighten up her plot. Nice for her to be remembered in that way.

She hadn't been to the graveyard for a while. It was just so impossibly bleak and devastating to stand there and look down at the headstone, knowing her daughter was…

She swallowed hard.

Don't even think it.

It hurt too much. Going to the grave just kept proving that she was dead, making Sydney feel helpless and lost—a feeling she couldn't bear. She'd found that by staying away, by existing in her dreams and her memories, she could still see her daughter alive and well and she never had to stare at that cold, hard, depressing ground any more.

Blinking back the tears, she was about to thank Mrs Courtauld when the computer screen that announced patient's names beeped into life and there was her name. Ms Sydney Harper. Dr Jones's room.

She got up quickly, then did a double-take, looking at the screen again. Dr *Jones?*

But she'd booked in with Dr Preston. *He* was her doctor, not this Jones person! And who was it? A locum? A new partner? If it was, and she'd been passed on to someone else…

She shoved her book back into her bag, wondering briefly if she ought to go and check with Reception and see what had happened, but the doctor was probably waiting. If she faffed around at Reception she might lose her appointment altogether—and she needed those tablets!

Clearing her throat, she pushed through the door and headed down the corridor. To the left, Dr Preston's room. To the right, Dr Jones's.

Sydney hesitated outside the door, her hand gripping the handle, afraid to go in. What if this new doctor wanted to *ask questions?* She wasn't sure she was ready to tell the story *again*. Not to a stranger. Dr Preston knew everything. There was no need to explain, no need for her to sit in front of him and embarrass herself by bursting into tears, because he *knew*. Knew what she'd gone through and was *still* going through. He often saw her in the village and would call out with a cheery wave, ask her how she was doing. She appreciated that.

A newcomer might not understand. A locum might be loath to hand out a prescription as easily.

Please don't ask me any probing questions!

She sucked in a breath and opened the door, not knowing what or who to expect. Was Dr Jones a woman? A man? Young? Old?

She strode in, her jaw set, determined to be as brief as possible so she could get her prescription and get out again but she stopped as her gaze fell upon the extremely handsome man seated behind the doctor's desk.

Her breath caught in her throat and somehow paralysed it. He was a complete shock to her system. Totally unexpected. It was like walking into a room expecting to see a normal person—some old guy in a boring shirt and tie...maybe someone bald, with old-fashioned glasses and drab brown trousers—but instead laying eyes upon a movie star in all his airbrushed glory.

The man was dressed in a well-fitting dark suit, with the brightest, bluest eyes she'd ever seen. There was a gorgeous smile of greeting upon his face. The type that stopped your heart. That stopped you breathing for a moment.

Oh, my!

Sydney had not noticed a good-looking man since Alastair had left. There was no point. Men were not on her radar. She wasn't looking for another relationship. What was the use? She'd only end up getting blamed for everything.

She was sure those men were out there. Somewhere. Even though Silverdale Village wasn't exactly overrun with hot guys. The type who ought to star in Hollywood movies or get their kits off for a charity calendar. She'd just never noticed. Living too much in her own head.

But *this* guy? Dr Jones?

I'm staring at him! Like a goldfish with my mouth hanging open! Speak, Sydney. Say something. Anything! So he knows he's not dealing with a mute.

She turned away from him to close the door, shutting her eyes to compose herself and take in a steadying breath. Hoping her cheeks had stopped flushing, hoping he hadn't noticed the effect he'd had on her.

He's just a guy.

Just.

A.

Guy.

She blew her breath out slowly before she turned around, telling herself to try and sound haughty and distant, whilst simultaneously feeling her cheeks flame hot enough to sizzle bacon. 'I…um…I don't mean to be rude, but I made an appointment to see Dr Preston…?'

An angel had walked into his consulting room.

An angel with long, luscious waves of chocolate-coloured hair and sad grey eyes. Big, sad eyes, tinged with red, in the fresh face of an English rose.

Startled, he dropped his pen, fumbling for it when it fell from his fingers and smiling in apology. What the hell had just happened? Why was he reacting like this? She was just a patient!

He'd not expected to feel suddenly...*nervous*. As if he'd never treated a patient before. Tongue-tied. Blindsided by his physical response to this woman. He could feel his normal greeting—*Morning, take a seat, how can I help?*—stifled in his throat and he had to turn to his computer, glancing at the screen briefly to gather his thoughts before he could speak.

Sydney Harper.

Beautiful. Enchanting.

A patient!

Reel your thoughts back in and show that you know what you're doing.

He cleared his throat. 'Er...yes, you did... But he...er...got overbooked.' He paused briefly, noticing the way she hovered uncertainly at the door. The way her long cardigan covered her almost to mid-thigh, the shapeless garment hiding any figure she might have. The way her heavy tartan skirt covered her legs down to her boots. The way her fingers twisted around each other.

Curious... Why is she so frightened? Why do

I get the feeling that she tries her best not to be noticed?

He could see her gaze darting about the room, as if she were looking for means of escape, and suddenly curiosity about this woman overrode any previous nervousness.

'Is that okay?'

'I'd prefer to see Dr Preston. He knows me. I'm *his* patient.'

Nathan glanced back at the computer, so that he wouldn't stare at her and make her feel even more uncomfortable. Did Dr Preston *really* know her? The last time she'd been into the surgery had been—he checked the screen—a year ago. A lot could change in a year.

He should know.

Forget that. Concentrate on your work.

He was itching to know what ailed her. What he could help her with. How to keep her in the room and not have her bolt like a skittish horse.

Purely on a professional basis, of course. I'm not interested in her in that *way.*

What had brought her to the surgery today?

She looked anxious. A bit stressed. Not entirely comfortable with this change.

He gave her his best friendly smile. 'Why don't you take a seat? You never know, I might be able to help. Doctors do that.' He tried to reassure her, but she approached the chair opposite him as if she were a gazelle trying to sidle past a ravenous lion.

He waited for her to sit and then he looked her over. A little pale, though her cheeks were flushed. Her pulse was probably elevated. Her blood pressure rising. What had made her so anxious? He was intrigued. But he'd learnt a valuable trick as a doctor. Silence was a wonderful tool. People would feel compelled to fill it. They'd start talking. Eventually.

So he waited, noting how white her knuckles were as they clutched the bag upon her lap.

And he waited.

She was looking at anything *but* him. Checking out the room as if it were new to her before she finally allowed herself to glance at his face. Her cheeks reddened in the most delightful way, and she was biting her bottom lip as she finally made eye contact.

'I need some sleeping pills. Dr Preston told me to come again if I needed a repeat.'

Ah. There we go!

'You're not sleeping well?'

Her cheeks reddened some more, and again she averted her eyes. 'Not really. Look, I'm needed back at work, so if you could just write me a prescription? I don't want to keep my clients waiting.'

Nathan Jones sat back in his swivel chair and appraised her. He was curious as to why she needed them. 'Sleeping pills are really a last resort. I'll need a few details from you first of all.'

The flash of alarm in her eyes was startling to observe. And if she twisted the strap of her handbag any more it would soon snap.

Sydney shook her head. 'I don't have long.'

'Neither do I. So let's crack on, shall we? Eight minutes per patient can go by in the blink of an eye.' He was trying to keep it loose. Casual. Nonthreatening. This woman was as taut as a whip.

She let out an impatient breath. 'What do you need to know?'

'Tell me about your sleep routine.'

Does your husband snore? Does he toss and turn all night, keeping you awake? Wait... What the...?

Why was he worrying about whether she had a husband or not? He wasn't looking to go *out* with this woman. She was a patient! At least for now. He had no doubt that the second she bolted from his consulting room she would make sure she never had to see him again!

'What about it?'

'Is it regular?'

'I work long days at the veterinary surgery across the road from here. I'm the only vet there, so I'm on call most nights, and since the new homes got built I've been busier than ever.'

'So you get called out a lot?'

'I do.'

He nodded and scribbled a note. 'And are you finding it difficult to drop off to sleep?'

'Yes.'

'Worried about your beeper going off? Or is it something else?'

She looked at him directly now. 'Look, Dr Preston has given me the pills before. I'm sure he won't mind if you give me some more.'

She didn't like him prying. He glanced at her records, his eyes scanning the previous note. Yes, she was correct. She'd been given sleeping pills by Dr Preston this time last year...

'*...due to the sudden death of the patient's daughter three years ago, patient requested tranquillisers...*'

He felt a lump of cold dread settle in his stomach as he read the notes fully.

She'd lost her *child*. Sydney Harper had lost her daughter and she couldn't sleep when the anniversary of her death got close. It happened every year. *Oh, heavens.*

He closed his eyes and gritted his teeth, mentally apologising.

'I...er...yes. I can see that in your notes.'

How terrible. The most awful thing that could ever happen to a parent. And it had happened to her and he was trying to poke around in her despair when it was clear in her notes why she needed the pills. But would he be being a good doctor just to give them to her? Or would he be a *better* doctor if he tried to stop her needing them? They could be addictive…

'I'm sure he won't mind if you give me some more tablets.'

Nathan had a daughter. Anna. She was six years old and she was all he had in this world. He couldn't imagine losing her. She was every-thing to him right now. What this poor woman had been through…! No wonder she looked the way she did.

'I can write you a prescription, but…' He paused. 'Have you ever been offered counsel-ling?'

She looked directly at him, her demeanour sug-gesting she was about to explain something to a child. 'I was. And I did go to start with. But it didn't help me so I stopped going.'

'Perhaps you weren't ready for it then. Would you be interested in trying it again now? It might help you with this sleeping issue. I could arrange it for you.'

The computer whirred out the prescription and he grabbed it from the printer and passed it over to her.

'Counselling is not for me. I don't…talk…about what happened.'

'Maybe that's the problem?' The words were out before he could censor them. He bit his lip with annoyance. Too late to take the words back. He needed to cover their crassness. And quickly. 'Have you tried a different night-time routine? Warm milk? A bath? That kind of thing?'

But she'd stood up, was staring down at him, barely controlling the anger he could see brewing behind her eyes. 'Are you a father, Dr Jones?'

He nodded solemnly, picturing his daughter's happy, smiling face. 'I am.'

'Have you ever experienced the loss of a child?'

He could see where she was going with this, and felt horrible inside. He looked away. 'No. Thankfully.'

'Then don't tell me that *warm milk*—' she almost spat the words '—will make me better.' She spun on her heel and when she got to the door, her hand on the handle, she paused, her head low, then glanced over her shoulder, her teeth gritted. 'Thank you for my prescription.'

Then she left.

He felt as if a hurricane had blown through the room.

He felt winded. Stunned. He had to get up and pace, sucking in a lungful of air, running both hands through his hair before he stood and stared out of the window at the sparrows and starlings trying to take food from the frozen feeders hanging outside. The smaller birds were carefully picking at the peanuts, whereas the starlings were tossing white breadcrumbs everywhere, making a mess.

No, he had *not* experienced the same pain that Sydney had gone through. He would never want to. But he *did* know what it felt like to realise that your life had changed for evermore.

People dealt with tragedies in different ways. Some found comfort in food. Some in drink or drugs. Some kept it all inside. Others found it easy to talk out their feelings and frustrations. A few would blindly choose to ignore it and pretend it had never happened.

He felt deflated now that she'd left his room. Sydney Harper was intense—yes—and hurting—definitely—but there was something about her. He couldn't quite put a finger on it.

It bothered him all day. Through seeing all his patients. The chest infection, the sprained ankle, a case of chicken pox, talking someone through using his asthma medication. His thoughts kept returning to his first patient at his new job.

Sydney Harper.

Beautiful. Elegant.

Fragile.

And then it came to him. The reason why he couldn't forget her. The reason he kept going over and over their interaction that morning.

I'm attracted to her.

The thought stopped him in his tracks. No. He couldn't—*wouldn't*—be. He had nothing to offer her. Besides, he had a child to take care of. Clearly!

No. That way danger lay.

He doubted he would ever see her again. Not as his *patient*. She had clearly wanted to see Dr Preston, and the way she'd stormed from the room had left him feeling a little bit stunned. He'd *never* had a patient walk out on him like that.

A fiancée, yes.

The mother of his child, yes.

But never a patient.

Sydney strode from the room feeling mightily irritated with Dr Jones, but not knowing why. Because she had the prescription she needed. She'd obtained what she'd wanted when she'd made the appointment. But now that she was out from under Dr Jones's interested, *unsettling* gaze she felt restless and antsy. Almost angry. As if she needed to go running for a few miles to get all of that uncomfortable adrenaline out of her system. As if she needed to burn off some of the inner turmoil she was feeling. As if she needed to let out a giant enraged scream.

Averting her gaze from the people in the waiting room, she went straight back to Reception and leant over the counter towards Beattie the recetptionist—the owner of a moggy called Snuggles.

'Beattie, I've just been seen by Dr Jones. Could

you make a note on my records that when I make an appointment to see Dr Preston—my *actual* doctor—that I should, indeed, *see* Dr Preston?'

Beattie looked up at her in surprise. 'You didn't *like* Dr Jones?'

Her jaw almost hit the floor.

'*Like* him? Liking him has nothing to do with it. Dr Preston is my GP and that is who I want to see when I phone to make an appointment!'

Beattie gave an apologetic smile. 'Sorry, Syd. Dr Jones offered to see you as Dr Preston was overrun and he knew you were in a rush to get back to work.'

Oh. Right. She hadn't thought of that. 'Well, that was very kind of him, but...'

It *had* been very kind of him, hadn't it? And what was she doing out here complaining? Even though she'd got what she needed.

Deflating slightly, she relaxed her tensed shoulders. 'Next time just book me in with Richard.'

'Will do. Anything else I can help you with?'

Not really. Though a niggling thought had entered her head... 'This Dr Jones that I saw today... Just a locum, is he? Just here for the day?'

She tried to make it sound casual. But it would be nice to know that she wouldn't be bumping into him in the village unless she had to. Not after she'd stormed out like that. That wasn't her normal behaviour. But something about the man had irritated her, and then he'd made that crass suggestion about warm milk...

'No, no. He's permanent.' Beattie's face filled with a huge grin. 'He moved to the village a week ago with his daughter. Into one of the homes on the new estate.'

'Oh. Right. Thank you.'

Permanent. Dr Jones would be living here. In Silverdale.

'Please don't tell me he's got an aging pet dog or anything?'

'I don't think so. But you'll run into him at the committee meetings for the Christmas market and the village nativity.'

What? She'd only just decided to return to those meetings. Had been looking forward to them!

'Why?'

Beattie looked at her oddly. 'Dr Preston is cutting down on his commitments now that he's nearly retired. He's asked Nathan to take over. You didn't like him? We all think he's gorgeous! Have you seen him smile? I tell you, that man's a heartbreaker!'

A heartbreaker? Not if *she* had anything to do with it.

Sydney grimaced, but thanked Beattie once again and left the surgery, pausing to wait for traffic to rush by so she could cross the road over to her own practice.

The new doctor was going to be on the Christmas committee. And she'd just agreed to go back. To help. She'd told them she would *be there*. Her heart sank at the thought of it as she neared her place of work.

Silverdale Veterinary Surgery was a relatively small building, comprised of two old cottages that had been knocked through inside and transformed from homes into a business.

Sydney loved it. It was clinical and business-like, but still retained its old-world charm with white walls and large exposed oak beams and, outside, a thatched roof. There were even window boxes, which she'd learnt to tend. They overflowed with primulas and pansies in the spring, but right now were hung with dark green ivy and indigo lobelia. And *no* fairy lights. Even if everyone else seemed to think it was okay to start decorating for Christmas in *November!*

She'd never been a green-fingered person. Not before she'd got married. But when Olivia came along the little girl had loved being in the garden and growing pretty things. Although Sydney had managed to kill the first few plants they'd got, they'd eventually learned together and their flowers had begun to thrive. There'd been nothing she'd liked better than to watch Olivia use her pink tin watering can to water them each evening, when it was cool. And Syd's talent with flowers had not gone unnoticed around the village either. She'd often been in charge of the flower stalls at the Christmas market each year.

When she'd been involved, anyway.

She pushed through the door and saw that her waiting room was pleasingly busy. There was Mr Shepherd, as expected, with his Great Dane, Sara with her new kitten, and no doubt in the box by Janet's feet were her two ferrets, Apollo and Zeus.

'Morning, everyone! Sorry to keep you waiting.'

Her anxiety was gone here. This was her home turf. Her safe haven. The place that *she* controlled. Was in charge of. Where there were no surprises. Well, nothing life-changing, anyway. Not to her. Here she could cure illnesses. Make things better. As much as she could.

Her clients waved and smiled and said good morning, too. They weren't too bothered about waiting for her. And she appreciated them for that.

In the staff room, she put on her green veterinary top and prepared to start work.

This was better.

This she could do.

This she was in control of.

Nathan stood in the playground, surrounded mostly by mothers waiting for their children to come out of infant school. As always, he felt like a complete fish out of water here. All the mothers stood in little groups, chatting and laughing. They all *knew* each other. And him…? He was the lone male, feeling awkward. Sure that he was standing out like a sore thumb.

He could feel their eyes on him. Judging him. Assessing him. Were they talking about him? Could they see his awkward gait? His limp? Could they see what was wrong with him? *It feels like they can.* He almost felt as if he was carrying a huge sign naming his condition around his neck.

Silverdale Infants had seemed the perfect place for Anna when he'd first come to the village for his job interview. He'd scouted the place out and asked the headteacher to give him a tour. He'd walked through the school with her, looking in the classrooms, seeing the happy children and their paintings, listening to them singing in assembly and watching as they'd sat for storytime in their impossibly small chairs. He'd genuinely felt his daughter would be happy there. It had a good vibe. The head was a nice woman and Miss Howarth, Anna's teacher-to-be, seemed really lovely and welcoming.

Nathan had just had his first day in his new job and this had been Anna's first day at her new school. He could only hope that it had gone as well as his own day, and that she would come running out with a big smile on her face. Then, perhaps, the lump of anxiety in his stomach would disappear and they'd be able to go home and he'd cook dinner.

Nathan hated being away from Anna. Giving her into the care of someone else. But he had to work and she had to learn—and weren't schools considered *in loco parentis?*

He was grateful for the flexible hours his new job afforded him. Since Gwyneth had left them he'd had to become both father *and* mother to Anna. And he didn't think he was doing too badly. Anna seemed happy enough, only occasionally asking why she didn't have a mummy, like other children. Those days were hard. When he could see the hurt in his daughter's eyes. And when it happened he would curse Gwyneth inwardly, whilst outwardly he would throw everything he had at making his daughter happy.

He just couldn't give her the mother that she

wanted. He wasn't ready to be with someone new. To open himself up to possible hurt and betrayal. To being left again. And why put Anna through the hope of getting to know someone when they might walk away and break her heart, too?

He didn't bad-mouth Gwyneth to Anna. It wasn't up to him to tell Anna how to feel about her mother. Anna might want to find her one day and see her. Talk to her. Ask her things. Did he want Anna to grow up resentful and hating her mother? No. Even if it was hard for him. Because Gwyneth had abandoned them both. And that hurt. Not so much now, but it still caused pain whenever he thought about his and Anna's future.

He sighed as he thought about his mistake in getting involved with Gwyneth. She'd been so much fun to begin with, but—as was sometimes the way with relationships—they'd both realised something was missing. And then they'd discovered she was pregnant…

Life was short. And he would not have Anna spending hers moping about for a mother who had no interest in her whatsoever. He was only sorry that he hadn't noticed Gwyneth's shallowness earlier on. Before he'd got in too deep.

The school bell rang and he braced himself. Now he'd know. Had it gone well?

Crossing his fingers in his jacket pockets, trying not to shiver in the late November cold, he looked for her familiar face amongst the mass of children pouring out through the door, all of them almost identical in their little green jumpers and grey skirts or trousers.

Then he saw her and his heart lifted.

'Daddy!'

She was *smiling.* Beaming at him as she ran to his open arms, clutching a painting that was still slightly wet. Nathan scooped her up, hefting her onto his hip, trying not to grimace at the pain in his shoulder.

'What do we have here?' He glanced at the painting. There were daubs of brown and green that he guessed was a tree, and to one side was a large black blob with ears. 'Is that Lottie?'

Anna nodded, grinning, showing the gap where her two front teeth were missing. 'Yes!'

Lottie was their pet rabbit and his one concession to Anna's demands to fill their house with pets of all shapes and sizes. Anna *adored* animals, and ever since she'd started at nursery had plagued him with requests for cats or dogs or parrots or anything that had fur, feathers or a cute face.

Knowing that they would both be out all day—him at work, she at school—he'd not thought a dog or a cat was appropriate, but he'd given in and allowed her a rabbit. It had the added bonus of living outdoors and its presence had stopped Anna from 'rescuing' injured insects and bringing them in to be 'nursed'.

'It looks just like her.' He squinted as he saw a small daub of bright orange. 'Is that a carrot?'

'No, Daddy. Silly! That's a worm.'

'Oh, right.' He gently placed his daughter back on the ground, being careful not to grimace or wrench himself further. 'So how did it go? Was it good? Did you make friends?'

She nodded. 'Lots and lots.'

She proceeded to list them as they walked back to the car. There seemed an *awful* lot, and to his ears it sounded as if she'd just memorised the register, but he nodded and smiled at her as she told him about Hattie with the bright pink glasses, and George who had held her hand as they'd walked to assembly.

They were soon home. Nathan still had half their life packed away in boxes after the move, but he knew they'd get there eventually. All the important stuff was unpacked. And Anna's room had everything. He'd done that first. Everything else could wait for when he had the time. He just had to decide where he wanted it all to go.

The house was brand-new, so had none of that old-world character the rest of the cottages in the village had. He had tiles on his roof, not thatch. A modern fake fireplace rather than an old rustic one with real flames. Flat, smooth walls rather than whitewashed ones with crooked oak beams.

Still, the place would get its character eventually.

'I'm going to see if Lottie missed me.' Anna ran through the house towards the back door, so she could go into the garden.

'Not yet, young lady,' he called after her. 'Go upstairs and get out of your uniform first.'

'Daddy, please!'

'It was raining this morning, Anna. I'm not having you getting your uniform covered in mud and straw. Please go and get changed.'

She pouted, but only briefly, and then she ran back past him, clambering up the stairs as he took their bags through to the kitchen, pinned her painting to the fridge with a magnet that was shaped like a banana. He'd picked up some vegetables from a farm shop, so he popped those in the fridge, then switched on the kettle for a drink.

Upstairs, he heard a small *thunk* as Anna kicked off her shoes and soon enough she was trotting back down the stairs, wearing a weird combination of purple corduroy skirt, green tee shirt and a rather loud orange and yellow cardigan.

'Nice... I'm liking your style.' He was keen to encourage her to wear what she wanted and to pick her own clothes. He'd learned that it was important—it helped Anna to develop her independence and allowed her to express herself. And he needed Anna to be a strong character. He wanted to encourage her at all times to feel happy about herself and her own decisions. To feel valued and beautiful. Because she *was* beautiful. With her mother's good looks but thankfully none of her character.

'Will you do me a juice, Daddy?'

'Sure thing, poppet.' He watched her twist the back door key and trot out into the garden. It wasn't huge out there, and as theirs was one of the original show houses it was just plain grass, with one side border of bushes. Nothing too impressive. Nothing that needed that much work. Something he figured he'd get to later. Maybe in the New Year.

But it had the rabbit hutch. The main reason for Anna to go and play outside. He was hoping to get her a trampoline, or a bike, or something. Maybe for Christmas.

He was just diluting orange juice with some water when he heard his daughter let out a blood-curdling scream.

'Daddy!'

'Anna?' His body froze, his heart stopped beating just for a millisecond, and then he was dropping the glass into the sink and bolting for the back door. What on earth had happened? Why had she screamed? Was she hurt?

Oh, please don't let her be hurt!

'Daddy!'

She ran into his arms, crying, and he held her, puzzled. What was it? Had she fallen over? What?

'Let me look at you.' He held her out at arm's length to check her over, but she looked fine. No scuffed knees, no grazes, no cuts. Just a face flooded with tears. What the…?

'Lottie's *bleeding*!' She pointed at the hutch before burying her face in his shirt.

He looked over the top of her head and could now see that the hutch had a broken latch and poor Lottie the rabbit sat hunched within, breathing heavily and audibly, with blood all over her and in the straw around her, as if she'd been involved in some sort of weird rabbit horror movie.

'Oh…' He stood up and led Anna away and back into the kitchen, sitting her down on one of the chairs by the table. 'Stay here.'

'She's bleeding, Daddy.'

'I know, honey. We'll need to take her to the vet.'

He didn't know if the poor thing might have to be put to sleep. There was a lot of blood, and Lottie looked like she might be in shock. He dashed for the cupboard under the stairs, where they'd put Lottie's carrier and got it out. Then he grabbed some latex gloves from under the sink and headed for the garden.

'I'll get Lottie. Can you get your shoes on for me? And your coat?'

'Where are we going?'

'The vet. The animal doctor. She'll need to check her over.'

'What if she dies, Daddy?' Anna sobbed, almost hiccupping her words.

He hadn't imagined this. He'd agreed to have Lottie knowing that rabbits lived for around ten years, hoping that they wouldn't have to face this day until Anna was in her teens. But not this early. Not *now*. He wasn't sure how she'd handle a pet's death at this age.

'Let's cross that bridge when we come to it. Get your shoes on. We need to get her there quickly.'

Nathan headed into the garden, slipped on the gloves and picked up the poor, shocked rabbit and placed her in the box. Normally she fought going in the carrier. But there was no fight today. His heart sank at the thought of having to tell his daughter her rabbit might die. Had Anna not been through enough?

He pulled off the bloodied gloves and quickly discarded them in the bin.

He could only hope that the veterinary surgery was still open.

CHAPTER TWO

IT HAD BEEN a long, tiring day. After her doctor's appointment Sydney had come back to the surgery and seen her first ten patients, and then she'd got round to her surgeries—a dental clean, two spays on cats, a dog to be neutered. Lunch had been quick, and then there had been more appointments: kitten visits, puppy checks, suture removals, an elderly dog that had had to be euthanised. Then she'd returned phone calls, given owners blood test results and now she was finishing off her paperwork. Filling in records. There were three animals being kept in overnight, but Lucy, her veterinary nurse, was giving them their final check before they left for the evening.

'I'll be ready to put my feet up tonight. Have you seen my ankles?' said Lucy.

Sydney smiled sympathetically. Lucy did seem to be suffering lately.

Almost all the lights were off, except for in her office and at the surgery entrance, and Sydney was just debating whether to have a cup of tea here or go home and have it there when she heard a loud banging on the surgery's front door.

A last-minute emergency?

She hurried through, switching on the lights as she went, and stopped when she saw who was on the other side of the door.

Dr Jones.

Oh.

Her pause was barely noticeable. At least she hoped so. Then she was rushing to the door, her cheeks flaming at having to let in the dishy doc. Though, judging by the look of worry on his face, he wasn't here to continue his conversation about warm milk.

She opened the door and Dr Jones came in, carrying a pet carrier. Behind him, a little uncertainly, followed a little girl with chestnut-brown hair in two ponytails held by pink bobbles, her face tearstained, pale and stunned. Seeing the little girl, so like Olivia—*no, so like her father*—

startled her and her stomach twisted painfully. As if she'd been punched in the gut.

She dragged her gaze away from the little girl and looked over at the doctor. 'Dr Jones? Can I help?'

Am I stammering? I feel like I'm stammering.

'My daughter's rabbit. I think it's been attacked.'

He lifted up the carrier, so she could see through the barred door, but it was impossible to gauge the extent of the animal's injuries.

Sydney glanced quickly at the little girl. She looked around Olivia's age. Maybe a bit older. She wasn't sure. But she was young, and she didn't need to see Sydney examining the rabbit if it was in a bad way. There were a lot of foxes out here in Silverdale Village. It was a very rural area, surrounded by farms and woodlands. Occasionally they even saw deer. The likelihood that there were animal predators around was very high.

All business now, she took the carrier from the doctor. 'Maybe your daughter should sit in the waiting room whilst I take a look?'

The little girl slipped her tiny hand into her father's. 'Don't leave me, Daddy.'

Dr Jones looked torn, but then he nodded. 'I'll sit with you.' He looked up at Sydney. 'Is that okay? If I sit out here with Anna?'

Anna. A lovely name.

'Of course. I'll just take a quick look.'

She hurried the rabbit through to the surgery, closing the door behind her and leaning back against it for a moment whilst she gathered herself.

That's Anna. Anna! Not Olivia.

The table where she usually examined pets had already been cleaned down, so she laid the carrier upon it and opened it up.

Inside was a very scared, very shocked black rabbit. From what she could see at this stage it had injuries to the top of its head, its left eye looked damaged, and there were other fine puncture marks across its back and legs. Sydney held it gently whilst she checked it over. The ears looked okay, as did its throat, and it seemed to be breathing fine, if a little loudly. She listened to its chest through her stethoscope and tried to get a better look at the eye, but she couldn't tell if it was ruptured or not.

Poor thing.

She suspected it might die of shock. She felt for its pulse. It was slow and faint, but that was typical for an animal like this in such a situation. Its gums were pale, too and its ears cool.

There wasn't much she could do at this point. Technically, she couldn't see any *fatal* injuries. The shock itself might be the killer here. All she could do at the moment was give the rabbit a painkilling injection and some antibiotics. But she'd need to check with Dr Jones first, in case they requested euthanasia.

Sydney put the rabbit back into the carrier and secured it, then headed to the waiting room, her own heart thumping rapidly at the thought of returning to speak to him.

'Dr Jones?'

He looked up when she called his name and then patted his daughter's hand and told her to stay in her seat before he came over to her and whispered in a low voice, 'How is she?'

Sydney also kept her voice low, not wanting to

upset Anna. 'She's in a great deal of shock. Can you tell me what happened?'

He shrugged. 'We're not sure. I'd been at work all day and then went to pick Anna up from school. She found Lottie like that when we got back.'

She nodded. 'She has sustained a great deal of damage to her left eye, but it's hard to see at the moment whether the eyeball itself has been ruptured. If it has, we might have to remove it, but at this stage I think we need to see if she'll survive the night.'

Dr Jones let out a heavy sigh and glanced at his daughter. 'Do you think Lottie might die?'

'It's fifty-fifty. I can give her a painkiller and some antibiotics if you wish. The bite marks are quite small and thin, possibly caused by a cat or a fox. Their mouths are filled with bacteria, so the chance of infection is high. There aren't any fatal injuries, but shock can kill an animal like this. It's up to you what measures you'd like me to take.'

She left the implication hanging. Did he want to see if the rabbit survived? Or did he want her to put the rabbit to sleep?

Dr Jones thought for a moment. 'Lottie is Anna's world. She loves animals. If there aren't any fatal injuries I think I owe it to her to see if Lottie makes it through the night. She won't be in any pain?'

'There'll be some discomfort, but the painkillers should help her an awful lot. I'll give her the injections, but if you can take her home, keep her somewhere warm and safe where she won't be disturbed. Do you have an indoor cage?'

He shook his head. 'I don't.'

'A bathroom, then. It's the safest place—somewhere there aren't any cables or wires to chew.'

'Will she want to eat?'

'You must get her to try. When a rabbit goes into shock it sometimes stops eating, and it will just lead to further complications if her digestive system shuts down. Offer her all her favourites and try to get her to drink, too. I'll need to see her first thing in the morning. Can you bring her in then?'

'Before surgery, yes. About eight?'

She nodded. 'I'll be here.'

Sydney slipped back inside her room and administered the injections. She really hoped on their behalf that Lottie would survive, but the poor thing had been through a terrible ordeal.

Back in the waiting room, she handed the carrier to Dr Jones and then, hesitantly, after thinking twice about doing so, she knelt in front of Anna. She tried not to notice the way the little girl's eyes looked into hers with so much hope. The way tears had welled in her eyes.

'Stay nice and quiet for her. No loud noises. Lottie needs to rest. Can you help her do that?'

Anna nodded. 'Yes.'

'Good.' She stood up again, frighteningly taken in by the little girl's big blue eyes. So similar to Olivia's it was unsettling. How was it possible that this little girl should remind her so strongly of her own?

Backing away, she held open the door for them, eager for them to go. So she could breathe again.

'What do I owe you?' Dr Jones glanced over at the till.

'We'll sort it in the morning. Don't worry. And good luck.'

She watched them go and backed away from

the door. They were a nice family, little Anna and her father. Was there a wife at home, waiting for news? It hadn't sounded like it. *He'd* been at work, *he'd* picked his daughter up from school. No mention of anyone else.

It doesn't matter. You're not interested in him anyway. Dr Jones is off limits!

So why was she thinking about him? Just because he was handsome? No. She wasn't that shallow. It must be because of the way she'd walked out on him that morning after her consultation. She'd been rude and had not apologised for it, either. She'd been defensive. Abrupt. Even though he had suggested the most ridiculous thing. And now she'd helped with their rabbit; that was all. They'd all had a shock and she knew how that felt. She wanted it to be easier for them.

Poor rabbit.

She hoped it was still alive in the morning.

Nathan had a sleepless night. It wasn't just because of the rabbit. Though he *was* worrying about getting up in the morning and finding her dead on the floor of the bathroom. If that happened then he wanted to deal with everything before Anna saw any of it. She shouldn't have to see that.

But, no. It was his own body that had kept him from sleeping.

Yesterday he'd tried to give advice on getting a good night's sleep to Sydney and he felt a bit hypocritical. Yes, there were tried and tested methods—relaxation, a milky drink, a warm bath, checking you had a comfortable bed—but they didn't work for him, either.

The spasticity he suffered from his multiple sclerosis kept *him* awake at night.

It wasn't as bad as it was for some people, and he knew he was lucky that no one just looking at him could guess his condition. He liked it that way. Fought to keep it so. But that didn't stop the damned stiffness that never seemed to go away. Sometimes he would lie there, trying to relax, and he would feel his muscles tightening so hard it almost felt like a vice. Then he would have to rub at his arm or his leg and hope that it would go away. It never did. And he knew it wouldn't. But that didn't stop him from trying.

So he'd spent the night alternately staring at the ceiling and getting up to check that the rabbit was still breathing.

At five a.m. he crawled out of bed, ready for a cup of tea, and checked on Lottie once more.

She's still alive. Thank goodness!

He gave her some dandelion leaves from the back garden and happily watched as she chewed them down, Her appetite was still good. Then he tried to pipette some water into her mouth—which she didn't like—so he decided to leave her a small bowl to drink from instead.

Anna was thrilled when she woke to find Lottie moving about in the bathroom. The rabbit's left eye still looked pretty mangled, though, and Anna was keen for the time to pass so she could go to the vet with her dad before school.

'You won't be at the vet, Anna. I'm dropping you at breakfast club, as normal.'

'But, Daddy, I want to go! Please?'

'No, Anna. I'm sorry.'

It was important that she kept to her routine. He hated changing things in Anna's life. And, though the incident with Lottie was out of the ordinary, it didn't mean that Anna's life had to be disturbed. It had changed enough already. Her mother had walked out on them both, not to mention that he had his diagnosis to deal with. Life for Anna would change dramatically at some point, if his condition worsened. Best to keep things as normal as he could, for however long he could. He would not have her upset unnecessarily.

Anna pouted for a bit, but got in the car happily and whispered good things to Lottie through the carrier door as he drove. 'You'll be okay, Lottie. The vet will take good care of you.'

With his daughter at breakfast club, Nathan drove to work, parked, and then walked across the road to the veterinary surgery with Lottie in her carrier once more. He was kind of proud of his daughter's little rabbit. Getting through a severe trauma and surviving. It was like finding a kindred spirit, and after getting up all night to check on her he felt he was bonding with her. And though last night he'd almost expected to have to tell Sydney to put Lottie to sleep, the fact that she'd lived… Well, he was kind of rooting for her now.

He was looking forward to seeing Sydney's re-action. She was an intriguing woman, and he was keen for her to see that the rabbit was still alive and find out her plan of action. But picturing the look of surprise on her face, or even trying to imagine what her smile might be like, was doing surprising and disturbing things to his insides. Things he didn't want to examine too closely for fear of what they might mean.

The bell above the door rang as he walked through, clutching the carrier, and he headed over to the reception desk, where a veterinary nurse sat.

'Lottie Jones to see Sydney, please.'

'Ah, yes. Please take a seat—you'll be called through in a moment.'

He sat and waited, his nerves strangely on edge. For the rabbit? For himself? For seeing Sydney again? Last night when he'd lain awake he'd thought about her a great deal. She was very beautiful, and totally out of his league, but…she intrigued him. For all that she'd been through—the loss of her daughter—she seemed surprisingly together. A little terse, maybe, but professional and she clearly cared for her animal charges.

What made her tick? What kept her going? Her bravery in the face of immense tragedy was a very positive force, and he liked to surround himself with positive people. He needed that; he tried to stay positive himself. Perhaps just by knowing her a little bit better he might learn her secret? If she ever forgave him for what he'd said. She was a strong woman. Determined. He could see that. The complete antithesis of Gwyneth.

He shook his head as he thought of his thoughtless advice to her. *Warm milk?*

So busy was he, feeling embarrassed for what he'd said, that he wasn't ready when she opened her surgery door and called his name. 'Dr Jones?'

He looked up, startled. Today, her long brown hair was taken up into a messy ponytail. There were little wavy bits hanging free around her face, and even without make-up she looked amazing. He quickly cursed himself for noticing.

He got up, loudly cleared his throat and took

the carrier through to her consulting room, determined to be distant and professional.

'She's still with us. Lottie survived the night.'

He placed the carrier onto her examination table and stood quite far back, as if the physical distance would somehow stop him stealing glances at her.

Her eyebrows rose in surprise. 'Okay. Let's have a look at her.'

He watched as Sydney's very fine hands opened the carrier and she gave Lottie a thorough assessment, listening to her chest and abdomen with her stethoscope, taking the rabbit's temperature, checking the bites and scratches and finally examining the wounded eye.

He tried not to take notice of the small beauty mark on Sydney's bared neck, her delicate cheekbones, or the way she bit her bottom lip as she concentrated. She had a very fine mouth. With full, soft-looking lips.

Dragging his eyes away from her mouth, he stared hard at Lottie. *Focus on the rabbit!*

'It's impossible for me to see if the eyeball itself has ruptured. The damage is too extensive.

But until the swelling goes down I don't think we should assume that it has. I'm going to prescribe antibiotic drops for her eye, more pain-killers, and a drug to keep her digestive system working which is an oral medicine. Rabbits don't like receiving oral meds, so if you can put the medicine in a food that you know she will eat you can get it into her that way.'

He nodded, keeping his gaze fixed firmly on Lottie's thick black fur so that he didn't accidentally start staring into Sydney's soft grey eyes. 'Okay. How often does she need the meds?'

'The eye drops three times a day, the oral meds four times a day. Will you be able to do that?'

He thought about his work schedule. It would be tough. But manageable. Perhaps if he kept Lottie in her carrier at work? In an unused room?

'I'll find a way.'

'I'll need to see her in about four days' time. The swelling should have gone down by then, we'll know if the antibiotics have worked, and I'll be able to see if the eye needs to be removed.'

He risked a glance at her wide almond-shaped eyes. 'She'd cope with that?'

'Not all rabbits do well with surgery, and if we do have to remove the eye then she could be susceptible to further infection. Keep it clean. Bathe it with cooled boiled water when you can—three or four times a day.'

'Like a proper patient.' He smiled and closed the door on the carrier once again. 'Thank you, Sydney, for seeing us last night. I appreciate that you were probably closed and your staff were ready to go home.'

She glanced away, her cheeks glowing slightly, before she began typing notes into her computer. 'It was no problem.'

He watched her where she stood by the computer. It was better with her further away and not looking at him. He could think more clearly. And he wanted to make things right between them. He hated it that she'd left his consulting room feeling stressed and angry. Hated it that he'd insulted her daughter's memory with a crass piece of advice.

'I'd like to thank you properly, if I may? We got off to a bad start the other day and... Well, we both live in this village. It'd be nice to know I've not upset the first person I got to properly meet.

Would you join me for a coffee some time? I'd really appreciate the chance to apologise.'

What on *earth are you doing?*

The invitation had just come out. He cursed himself silently, knowing she would refuse him, but, hell, he kind of wanted her to say *yes*. He couldn't just see her about rabbits and sleeping tablets. Part of him wanted to know more about her. About that strong side of her that kept her going in the cruel world that had taken her daughter. That inner strength of hers…

But he also got the feeling that if they were given the chance the two of them might become friends. It had been a long time since he'd sat down and just chatted with a woman who wasn't a patient, or some cashier in a shop, someone with whom he could pass the time of day.

'Oh, I don't know. I—' She tucked a stray strand of hair behind her ear and continued typing, her fingers tripping over one another on the keyboard, so that he could see she had to tap 'delete' a few times and go back, cursing silently.

He focused on her stumbling fingers. Tried not to imagine himself reaching for her hands and stilling them. 'Just coffee. I don't have an evil plan to try and seduce you, or anything.'

Shut up, you idiot. You're making it worse!

Now she looked at him, her hands frozen over the keys. Her cheeks red. Her pause was an agonising silence before her fingers leapt into life once more, finishing her notes before she turned to him and spoke.

'That's kind of you, but—'

'Just a chat. Anna and I don't really know anyone here, and—well, I'd really like to know you.' He smiled. 'As a friend.'

It could never be anything else. Despite the fact that she was the most beautiful creature he had ever seen. Despite the fact that he could see her pulse hammering away in her throat. That her skin looked so creamy and soft. That he wanted to lift that stray strand of hair from her face and…

'I—'

'No pressure. Not a date. Just…coffee.'

He realised he was rambling, but he was confused. *She* confused him. Made him feel like he was tripping over his own words even though he wasn't. Made him surprised at what came out of his own mouth.

He'd not reached out to a woman like this since Gwyneth had left. He'd tried to become accustomed to the fact that he would spend the rest of his life alone. That he would not parade a stream of women past Anna. That he would not endanger his heart once again because on the one occasion he had given it to a woman she had ripped it apart.

The only female who would have his undying love was his daughter.

Which was as it should be.

Anna didn't need the huge change that a woman in their lives would bring. He was lucky that Gwyneth had left before Anna knew who she was or formed a bond.

But he missed being able just to sit with a woman and chat about everyday things. He missed asking about another person's day. He missed having adult company that didn't involve talks about unusual rashes, or a cough that wouldn't go away, or *could you just take a look at my boil?* And he imagined that Sydney would be interesting. Would have intelligent things to say and be the complete opposite of his ex-fiancée.

That was all he wanted.

All he *told* himself he wanted.

He waited for her to answer. Knowing she would turn him down, knowing it would hurt for some reason, but knowing that he'd had to ask because… Well, because he'd said something stupid to her the other day and he needed to apologise in the only way he knew how.

He waited.

Just a coffee?

Was there really such a thing as 'just a coffee' when a guy asked you out?

Because that was what he was doing. Asking her out. Like on a date. Right? And though he said there was no pressure, there was *always* pressure. Wasn't there?

Besides, why would she want to meet him for a drink? For a chat? This was the man who had got her so riled up yesterday, what with his probing questions and his damned twinkling eyes.

Did he not know how attractive he was? Because he seemed oblivious to it. Either that or he was a great actor. With great hair, and an irresistible charm about him, and the way he was looking at her right now… It was doing unbelievable things to her insides. Churning her up, making her stomach seem all giddy, causing her heart to thump and her mouth to go dry. She hadn't felt this way since her schoolgirl crush had asked her to the local disco. And her hands were trembling. *Trembling!*

Why had he asked her out? Why did he want to go for coffee? She had nothing to talk to him about. She didn't know this guy. Except that he was a hot doctor with effortlessly cool hair and eyes that melted her insides every time he smiled at her. Oh, and that he had a daughter. A beautiful little girl who seemed very lovely indeed, but who made her feel uncomfortable because she reminded her too much of Olivia.

If he wanted to apologise to her then why didn't he just do it? It wouldn't take a moment. No need for them to go to a coffee shop. He could say it here. Now. Then she could thank him, and then he could go, and it would all be over.

Why would she get any kind of involved with this man? He was dangerous in so many ways. Intelligent, good-looking, attractive. Not to mention his adorable daughter… She pushed the thought away. *No.*

She wanted to say, *We have nothing to talk about.* She wanted to say, *But there's no point.* She wanted to yell, *You're so perfect you look airbrushed. And I can't have coffee with you because you make me feel things that I don't want to feel and think of things I sure as hell don't want to think about!*

But she said none of those things. Instead she found herself mumbling, 'That'd be great.' Her voice almost gave out on that last word. Squeaking out of her closed throat so tightly she wondered if only dogs would have been able to hear it.

Oh, no, did I just agree to meet him?

The goofy smile he gave her in return made her temperature rise by a significant amount of degrees, and when he said goodbye and left the room she had to stand for a minute and fan her face with a piece of paper. She berated herself inwardly for having accepted. She would have to turn him down. Maybe call the surgery and leave a message for him.

This was a mistake.

A big mistake.

Nathan waited for his computer system to load up, and whilst he did he sat in his chair, staring into space and wondering just what the hell he had done.

Sydney Harper had said yes to his coffee invitation.

Yes!

It was unbelievable. There must have been some spike, some surge in the impulse centre of his brain that had caused his mind to short circuit or something. His leg muscles would sometimes spasm and kick out suddenly—the same must have happened with his head. And his mouth.

He had no doubt that they would get on okay. She would show up—a little late, maybe—pretend that she couldn't stay for long, have some excuse to leave sooner than she'd expected. Maybe even get a friend to call her away on an invented emergency. But…they'd get on okay. He'd apologise right away for what he'd said. Be polite as could be.

Surely it was a good thing to try and make friends when you moved to a new area? That was all he was doing.

And how many guys have you invited for coffee?

The only people he really knew in Silverdale were Dr Preston, some of the staff at the medical centre and his daughter's teacher at school, and they were more colleagues than actual friends. He'd left all his old friends behind when he'd moved from the city to this remote village. They kept in touch online. With the odd phone call and promises to meet up.

Sydney could be a *new* friend. A female friend. That was possible. How could it *not* be in today's modern age? And once he got past her prickly demeanour, made her realise he was sorry and showed her that he was no threat to her romantically, then they could both relax and they would get on like a house on fire.

He had no doubt of that.

So why, when he thought of spending time with Sydney, did he picture them kissing? Think of himself reaching for her hand across the table and lifting it to his lips while he stared deeply into her eyes. Inhaling the scent of her perfume upon her wrist…

And why did that vision remind him of Gwyneth's twisted face and her harsh words?

'I can't be with you! Why would anyone want to be with you? You're broken. Faulty. The only thing you can offer is a lifetime of pain and despair and I didn't sign up for that!'

Determined not to be haunted by his ex-fiancée's words, he angrily punched the keys on his keyboard, brought up his files and called in his first patient of the day.

Sam Carter was a thirty-two-year-old man who had just received a diagnosis of Huntington's Disease. His own father had died from it quite young, in his fifties, and the diagnosis had been a terrible shock to the whole family after Sam had decided to have genetic testing. Now he sat in front of Nathan, looking pale and washed out.

'What can I do for you, Sam?'

His patient let out a heavy sigh. 'I dunno. I just...need to talk to someone, I guess. Things are bad. At home. Suddenly everything in my life is about my diagnosis, and Jenny, my wife... Well...we'd been thinking about starting a family and now we don't know what to do and...'

Nathan could see Sam's eyes reddening as he fought back tears. Could hear the tremor in his patient's voice. He understood. Receiving a diagnosis for something such as Huntington's was very stressful. It changed everything. The present. The future. His own diagnosis of multiple sclerosis had changed *his* life. And Anna's. It had been the final axe to fall on his farce of a relationship.

'What did your consultant say?'

Sam sniffed. 'I can't remember. Once he said the words—that I had Huntington's—I didn't really hear the rest. I was in shock... He gave us leaflets to take home and read. Gave us some websites and telephone numbers of people who could help, but...' He looked up at Nathan and met his eyes. 'We wanted to start a *family!* We wanted babies! And now... Now we don't know if we should. Huntington's is a terrible disease, and I'm not sure I want to pass that on to my children.'

Nathan nodded. It was a difficult thing to advise upon as a general practitioner. He didn't have a Huntington's specialty. He didn't want to give Sam the wrong advice.

'I hear what you're saying, Sam. It's a difficult situation and one that you and your wife must come to an agreement about together. I'm sure your consultant could discuss giving you two genetic counselling. A counsellor would be able to advise you better about the possibility of passing Huntington's to your children and what your options might be in terms of family planning. Have you got another appointment scheduled with your consultant soon?'

'In a month.'

'Good. Maybe use the time in between then and now to think of what questions you want to ask him. Just because you have Huntington's, and your father did too, it does not mean that any children you and Jenny have, will develop it. It's a fifty per cent chance.'

'They could be carriers, though.'

'That's a possibility, yes. Your consultant will be much better placed to talk this over with you, but if I'm right CVS—chorionic villus sampling—can be used to gain some foetal genetic material and test for the disease. And I believe there's also a blood test that can be performed on Jenny to check the cell-free foetal DNA, and that would carry no risk of miscarriage. How are you coping on a day-to-day level?'

'Fine, I guess. I have a chorea in my hand sometimes.' A chorea was a hand spasm. 'But that's all, so far.'

Nathan nodded. 'Okay. What about sleeping? Are you doing all right?'

'Not bad. I've lost some sleep, but I guess that's down to stress. My mind won't rest when I go to bed.'

'That's understandable. If it gets difficult then come and see me again and we'll look at what we can do.'

'How long do you think I've got, Dr Jones? My dad died young from this; I need to know.'

Nathan wanted to reassure him. Wanted to

tell him that he would live a long life and that it would all be fine. But he couldn't know that. He had no idea how Sam's Huntington's would affect him. It affected each sufferer differently. Just like multiple sclerosis did.

'It's impossible to say. You've just got to take each day as it comes and live it the best you can. Then, whenever the end does arrive, you'll know you lived your life to the fullest.'

Sam smiled. 'Is that *your* plan, Doc?'

Nathan smiled back. It certainly was. Living his life and trying to be happy was his number one aim. And he wanted the people around him to be happy too. The fact that he'd upset Sydney the way he had… Perhaps that was why he had asked her to coffee.

'It is.'

Sydney stared at her reflection in the mirror. 'What on earth am I doing?' she asked herself.

Her make-up was done to perfection. Her eyeliner gave a perfect sweep to the gentle curve of her eyelid. The blusher on her cheeks highlighted her cheekbones and her lipstick added a splash of colour, emphasising the fullness of her lips. Her eyelashes looked thicker and darker with a coating of mascara, making her grey eyes lighter and clearer. Her normally wavy hair had been tamed with the help of some styling spray, and the earrings in her ears dangled with the blue gems that had once belonged to her grandmother.

She looked completely different. Done up. Like a girl getting ready for a date. Like a girl who was hoping that something might happen with a special guy.

It's just coffee! Why have you put in this much effort? Is it for him?

Grabbing her facial wipes, she rubbed her face clean, angry at herself, until her skin was bare and slightly reddened by the force she'd used upon it. She stared back at her new reflection. Her normal reflection. The one she saw every day. The one bare of pretence, bare of cosmetics. Mask-free.

This is me.

She was *not* getting ready for a date! This was coffee. Just coffee. No strings attached. They were just two people meeting. Associates. She did *not* have to get all dressed up for a drink at The Tea-Total Café.

So she pulled the dress off over her head and put on her old jeans—the ones with the ripped knees—slipped on a white tee and then an over-sized black fisherman's jumper and scooped her hair up into a scruffy bun, deliberately pulling bits out to give a casual effect. Then she grabbed her bag, thick coat and scarf and headed out, figuring that she'd walk there. It wasn't far. The wind might blow her hair around a bit more. She would *not* make any effort for Dr Jones.

Striding through the village, she hoped she looked confident, because she wasn't feeling it. She had more nerves in her stomach now than she'd had taking her driving test or her final exams. Her legs were weak and her nerves felt as taut as piano strings.

It was all Dr Jones's fault—that charming smile, those glinting blue eyes, that dark chestnut hair, perfectly tousled, just messy enough to make it look as if he hadn't touched it since rolling out of bed.

She swallowed hard, trying *not* to think of Dr

Jones in bed. But Sydney could picture him perfectly...a white sheet just covering his modesty, his naked body, toned and virile as he gazed at her with a daring smile...beckoning her back beneath the sheets...

Stop. It.

She checked her mobile phone. Had the surgery been in touch? A last-minute patient? An emergency surgery, maybe? Something that would force her to attend work so she didn't have to go? But, no. Her phone was annoyingly clear of any recent messages or texts. She was almost tempted to call the surgery and just check that things were okay—make sure no cows on the nearby farms were about to calve. Right now she'd be much happier standing in a swamp of mud or manure with her arm in a cow's insides. Instead she was *here*.

She stood for a moment before she entered, psyching herself up.

The bell above the door rang as she went inside and she was met by a wall of heat and the aroma of freshly brewed coffee and pastries. Praying he wouldn't be there, she glanced around, ready to flash a smile of apology to the staff behind the counter before she ducked straight out again— but there he was. Dashing and handsome and tie- less, dressed in a smart grey suit, the whiteness of his shirt showing the gentle tan of his skin.

He stood up, smiling, and raised a hand in greeting. 'Sydney. You made it.'

Nervous, she smiled back.

Dr Jones pulled a chair out for her and waited for her to sit before he spoke again. 'I wasn't sure what you'd like. What can I get you?'

He seemed nervous.

'Er...just tea will be fine.'

'Milk and sugar?'

She nodded, and watched as he made his way over to the counter to place her order. He looked good standing there. Tall, broad-shouldered. Syd- ney noticed the other women in the café checking him out. Checking *her* out and wondering why she might be with him.

You can have him, ladies, don't worry. There's nothing going on here.

He came back moments later with a tray that

held their drinks and a plate of millionaire's shortbread.

She was surprised. 'Oh. They're one of my favourites.'

He looked pleased. 'Mine too. Help yourself.'

She focused on making her tea for a moment. Stirring the pot. Pouring the tea. Adding sugar. Adding milk. Stirring for a while longer. Stopping her hand from shaking. Then she took a sip, not sure what she was supposed to be talking about. She'd been quite rude to this man. Angry with him. Abrupt. Although, to be fair, she felt she'd had reason to be that way.

'So, how long have you lived in Silverdale?' he asked.

I can answer that.

'All my life. I grew up here. Went to the local schools. I left to go to university, but came back after I was qualified.'

She kept her answer short. Brief. To the point. She wasn't going to expand this. She just wanted to hear what he had to say and then she would be gone.

'And you now run your own business? Did you start it from scratch?'

'It was my father's business. He was a vet, too.'

'Does he still live locally?'

'No. My parents moved away to be closer to the coast. They always wanted to live by the sea when they retired.'

She paused to take another sip of tea, then realised it would be even more rude of her if she didn't ask *him* a question.

'What made you come to live in Silverdale?'

'I grew up in a village. Loved it. Like you, I left for university, to do my medical training, and then after Anna was born I decided to look for a country posting, so that Anna could have the same sort of childhood I had.'

She nodded, but knew he was glossing over a lot. Where was Anna's mother? What had happened? Anna wasn't a baby any more. She was five years old, maybe six. Was this his first country posting?

Who am I kidding? I don't need to know.

Sydney gave him a polite smile and nibbled at one of the shortbreads.

'My name's Nathan, by the way.'

Nathan. A good name. Kind. She looked him up and down, from his tousled hair to his dark clean shoes. 'It suits you.'

'Thanks. I like *your* name, too.'

The compliment coupled with the eye contact was suddenly very intense and she looked away, feeling heat in her cheeks. Was it embarrassment? Was it the heat from the café's ovens and the hot tea? She wasn't sure. Her heart was beginning to pound, and she had a desperate desire to start running, but she couldn't do that.

Nor could she pretend that she was relaxed. She didn't want to be here. She'd said yes because he'd put her on the spot. Because she hadn't been able to say no. Best just to let him know and then she could go.

She leaned forward, planting her elbows on the desk and crossing her arms in a defensive posture.

'You know…this isn't right. *This*. Meeting in a coffee shop. With you. I've been through a lot and you…' she laughed nervously '…you make me *extremely* uncomfortable. When I met you yesterday, in your surgery, I was already on edge. You might have noticed that. What with your doctor's degree and your—' she looked up '—your incredible blue eyes which, quite frankly, are ridiculously much too twinkly and charming.'

She stood, grabbing her bag and slinging it over her shoulder.

'I'm happy to help you with your daughter's rabbit, and I'll be the consummate professional where that poor animal is concerned, but *this*?' She shook her head. 'This I cannot do!'

She searched in her bag to find her purse. To lay some money on the table to pay for her tea and biscuit. Then she could get out of this place and back to work. To where she felt comfortable and in control. But before she could find her purse she became aware that Nathan had stood up next to her and leaned in, enveloping her in his gorgeous scent.

'I'm sorry.'

Standing this close, with his face so near to hers, his understanding tone, his non-threatening manner, his apology... There was nothing else she could do but look into his eyes, which were a breathtaking blue up close, flecked with tones of green.

She took a step back from his gorgeous proximity. 'For what?'

'For what I said to you. In our consultation. My remark was not intended to insult you, or the memory of your daughter, by suggesting that you could get over it with the help of...' he swallowed '...warm milk. But you were my first patient, and I knew you were in a rush, and I got flustered and...' His voice trailed off as he stared into her eyes.

Sydney quickly looked away, aware that the other customers in the café might be watching them, sensing the tension, wondering what was going on.

'Sydney?'

She bit her lip, her cheeks flushing, before she turned back to meet his gaze. 'Yes?'

'I promised this was just coffee. We've had tea and shortbread which may have changed things slightly, but not greatly. So please don't go. We're just drinking tea and chomping on shortbread. Please relax. I'm not going to jump your bones.'

'Right.' She stared at him uncertainly, imagining him *actually* jumping her bones, but that was too intense an image so, giving in, she sank back into her seat and broke off a piece of shortbread and ate it.

Her cheeks were on fire. This was embarrassing. She'd reacted oddly when all he'd expected was a drink with a normal, sane adult.

She glanced up. He was smiling at her. She hadn't blown it with her crazy moment. By releasing the steam from the pressure cooker that had been her brain. He was still okay with her. It was all still okay. He wasn't about to commit her to an asylum.

'I'm out of practice with this,' she added, trying to explain her odd behaviour. 'Could you please pretend that you're having tea with a woman who behaves normally?'

He picked up his drink and smiled, his eyes twinkling with amusement. 'I'll try.'

She stared back, uncertain, and then she smiled too. She hadn't scared him off with her minirant—although she supposed that was because he was a doctor, and doctors knew how to listen when people ranted, or nervously skirted around the main issue they wanted to talk about. Nathan seemed like a good guy. One who deserved a good friend. And good friends admitted when they were wrong.

'I'm sorry for walking out on you like that yesterday.'

'It's not a problem.'

'It is. I was rude to you because I was unsettled. I thought you were going to ask questions that I wasn't ready to answer and I just wanted to get out of there.'

'Why?'

'Because you made me nervous.'

'Doctors make a lot of people nervous. It's called White Coat Syndrome.'

She managed a weak smile. 'It wasn't your white coat. You didn't have one.'

'No.'

'It was you. *You* made me nervous.'

He simply looked at her and smiled. He was understanding. Sympathetic. Kind. All the qualities she'd look for in a friend.

But he was also drop-dead gorgeous.

And she wasn't sure she could handle *that*.

CHAPTER THREE

HE WAS SITTING there trying to listen to Sydney, hearing her telling stories of veterinary school and some of the cases she'd worked on, but all he could think about as he sat opposite her was that she was so very beautiful and seemed completely unaware of it.

It was there even in the way she sat. The way she held her teacup—not using the handle but wrapping her hands around the whole cup, as if it was keeping her warm. The way her whole face lit up when she laughed, which he was beginning to understand was rare. He'd wondered what she would look like when she smiled and now he knew. It was so worth waiting for. Her whole face became animated, unburdened by her past. It was lighter. Purer. Joyous. And infectious. Dangerously so.

And those eyes of hers! The softest of greys, like ash.

He was unnerved. He really had just wanted to meet her for this drink and clear the air after yesterday's abrupt meeting in his surgery. And to thank her for helping Lottie after her attack. But something else was happening. He was being sucked in. Hypnotised by her. Listening to her stories, listening to her talk. He liked the sound of her voice. Her gentle tone.

He was trying—*so hard*—to keep reminding himself that this woman was just going to be a friend.

Sydney worked hard. Very hard. All her tales were of work. Of animals. Of surgeries. She'd not mentioned her daughter once and he knew *he* couldn't. Not unless she brought up the subject first. If she wanted to share that with him then it had to be *her* choice.

He understood that right now Sydney needed to keep the conversation light. This was a new thing for her. This blossoming friendship. She was like a tiny bird that was trying its hardest not to be frightened off by the large tom cat sitting watching it.

'Sounds as if you work very hard.'

She smiled, and once again his blood stirred. 'Thank you. I do. But I enjoy it. Animals give you so much. Without agenda. Unconditionally.'

'Do you have pets yourself? It must be hard not to take home all the cases that pull at your heart strings.'

'I have a cat. Just one. She's ten now. But she's very independent—like me. Magic does her own thing, and when we both get home after a long day she either curls up on my lap or in my bed.'

Her face lit up as she spoke of Magic, but she blushed as she realised she'd referenced her bed to him.

A vision crossed his mind. That long dark hair of hers spread out over a pillow. Those almond-shaped smoky eyes looking at him, relaxed and inviting, as she lay tangled in a pure white sheet...

But he pushed the thought away. As lovely as Sydney was, he couldn't go there. This was friendship. Nothing else. He had Anna to think about. And his health.

He had no idea for how long he would stay relatively unscathed by his condition. His MS had been classified as 'relapsing remitting multiple sclerosis'. Which meant that he would have clear attacks of his symptoms, which would slowly get better and go away completely—until the next attack. But he knew that as the disease progressed his symptoms might not go away at all. They would linger. Stay. Get worse with each new attack, possibly leaving him disabled. But he was holding on to the thought that it wouldn't happen soon. That he would stay in relative good health for a long time.

But he could not, in any good conscience, put anyone else through that. Who deserved that?

And he had a child to think about. A child who had already lost her mother because of him. Who did not know what it was like to have that kind of female influence in her life. Bringing someone home would be a shock to Anna. It might upset her. It might bring up all those questions about having a mother again.

Sydney Harper was just going to be his *friend*. That was all.

He smiled as she talked, trying not to focus all of his attention on her mouth, and pushed thoughts of what it would be like to kiss her completely out of his head.

Later, he offered to walk her back to work.

'Oh, that's not necessary. You don't have to do that,' she protested.

'I might as well. I'm heading that way to pick up my pager as I'm on call tonight.'

She nodded her reluctant acceptance and swung her bag over her shoulder. Together they exited into the street.

It was a cold November day. With blue skies, just a few wispy white clouds and a chill in the air when they moved into the shade and lost the sun.

They walked along together, respectfully a few inches apart. But she was *so* aware of him and trying her hardest not to be.

Nathan Jones was delicious. Of course she was physically attracted to him. Who wouldn't be? Aside from his good looks, this man was intelligent. A good listener. Not at all judgemental. He'd seemed really interested in her. He'd asked

questions without being too probing and really
paid attention to her answers.

She was very much aware that although they
had just spent an hour in each other's company
she still didn't know much about him. They'd
both edged around serious subjects. They'd both
avoided talk of past traumas and upsets. And
they'd both kept everything light. Unthreatening.
No mention of the baggage that each of them had
to be carrying.

She liked that about him. It was as if he knew
what she needed.

She frowned, spotting someone from the local
council up a ladder, arranging the Christmas
lights. 'It gets earlier and earlier each year.'

Nathan nodded. 'I love Christmas.'

She certainly didn't want to talk to him about
that!

She changed the subject. 'Do you know your
way around Silverdale yet?' she asked him, aware
that the village had many tiny roads, closes and
cul-de-sacs. And now, with the new build of over
two hundred new homes on the edge of Silver-

dale, a lot of new roads had popped up that even *she* was unfamiliar with.

'Not really. But the GPS system in the car helps.'

'If you ever need help finding your way I could help you out. I know most places. Just pop in and ask at the desk.'

He looked at her. 'Thanks. If I ever get a call-out to the middle of nowhere I'll be sure to call in and pick you up first.'

Sydney glanced at him quickly, then looked away. That was a joke, surely? She'd meant that he could call in to her *work* and ask whoever was on Reception.

She felt his gaze upon her then, and she flushed with heat as they came to a stop outside her veterinary practice.

'Well, thank you for the tea. And the shortbread.'

'It was my pleasure.'

'I'll see you at the end of the week? When you bring in Lottie again?' she added.

The rabbit was due another check-up, so she

could look at its eye and see if it needed removing or not.

'Hopefully I'll see you before that.'

Her heart pounded in her chest. What did he mean?

'Why?'

'Because we're friends now, and friends see each other any time—not just at preordained appointments.' He smiled and held out his hand.

She blushed. 'Of course.'

She took his hand in hers and tried to give him a firm handshake, but she couldn't. All she could think of was that he was touching her. And she him! And that his hand felt warm and strong. Protective. It felt good, and she briefly imagined what it might feel like if he pulled her into his arms and pressed her against his chest.

He let go, and when he did she felt an odd sense of disappointment.

Now, why am I feeling that?

She stared back at him, unsure of how to say goodbye to this new friend. Should she give a small wave and go inside? Should they just say goodbye and walk away? Or should there be some sort of kiss on the cheek?

But if I kissed him and liked it...

'Well...maybe I'll see you later, then?'

He nodded. 'Yes.'

'Right. Bye.'

'Goodbye, Sydney.'

And then, with some hesitation, he leaned in and kissed the side of her face.

She sucked in a breath. His lips had only brushed her cheek, and were gone again before she could truly appreciate it, but for the millisecond he'd made contact her body had almost imploded. Her heart had threatened to jump out of her chest. Her face must have looked as red as a stop sign.

She watched him turn and walk across the road to his place of work and she stood there, breathing heavily, her fingers pressed to her face where his lips had been, and wondered what the hell she was doing.

With this *friendship* with Dr Nathan Jones.

Technically, they hadn't done *anything*. Just

shared a pot of tea. A plate of shortbread. A quick chat and a walk to work.

But all she could think of was how he'd looked when he'd smiled at her. His beautiful blue eyes. The way he'd listened, the way he'd filled the space of the cafeteria chair, all relaxed and male and virile. How attracted she was to him physically. How his lips had felt…and how frightened that made her feel.

Sydney turned and went into her own place of work.

She needed to cool down.

In more ways than one.

And she needed to stay away from Dr Nathan Jones. He was going to be trouble.

The kiss had been an impulse. To fill an awkward pause. It was just what he did when he left female friends or relatives. He kissed them goodbye.

It didn't *mean* anything. The fact that he'd breathed in her scent as he'd leaned in…the fact that his lips had felt scorched the second they'd touched her soft cheek…the fact that he'd got a shot of adrenaline powerful enough to launch an armada meant nothing.

Did it?

It was just that it was something new. A new friendship. The fact that she was the most stunningly beautiful woman he'd met in a long time had nothing to do with it. He felt for her. She'd been through a trauma. The loss of a daughter was something he simply couldn't imagine. The fact that she was still standing, smiling and talking to people was a miracle, quite frankly. He couldn't picture going through that and having the power or strength to carry on afterwards. And she was so nice! Easy to talk to. Friendly once you got past that prickly exterior she'd erected. But he could understand why that was there.

What he felt for her was protective. That was all. And didn't friends look out for one another?

Crossing the road, he called in to the surgery and picked up his pager for the evening, along with a list of house calls that needed to be completed before he had to pick up Anna at three-thirty. He had a good few hours' worth of work ahead of him, but he was distracted.

A simple coffee had been something else.

And he was afraid to admit to himself just what it had been.

Sydney sat hunched up on her couch, clutching a mug of cold tea and worrying at a loose bit of skin on her lip. Behind her head lay Magic the cat, asleep on the back of the couch, her long black tail twitching with dreams. The house was silent except for the ticking of the clock in the hallway, and Sydney's gaze was upon the picture of her daughter in the centre of the mantelpiece.

In the picture Olivia was laughing, smiling, her little hands reaching up to catch all the bubbles that her mum was blowing through a bubble wand.

She could remember that day perfectly. It had been during the summer holiday before Olivia was due to start school and it had been a Sunday. Alastair—Sydney's husband and Olivia's father—had gone to the supermarket to do a food-shop and Sydney and Olivia had been playing in the back garden. Her daughter had been so happy. Chasing bubbles, giggling. Gasping when

Sydney made a particularly large one that had floated up higher and higher until it had popped, spraying them with wetness. She'd been chasing down and splatting the smaller ones that she could reach.

'Mummy, look!' she'd said when she'd found a bubble or two resting on her clothes.

Sydney remembered the awe and excitement in her daughter's eyes. They'd been happy times. When they'd all believed that life for them was perfect. That nothing could spoil it. Olivia had been about to start infant school; Sydney had been going back to work full-time. It had been their last summer together. The last summer they'd enjoyed.

Before it had all changed. Before it had all gone dreadfully wrong.

Why did I not listen when she told me she had a headache?

She tried to keep on remembering that summer day. The sound of her daughter's deep-throated chuckles, the smile on her face. But she couldn't.

Every time she allowed herself to think of Olivia her thoughts kept dragging her back to that morning when she'd found her unconscious in her bed. To the deadly silence of the room except for her daughter's soft, yet ragged breaths. To the dread and the sickness in her stomach as she'd realised that something was desperately, deeply wrong. That her daughter wouldn't wake up no matter how much Sydney called her name. To the moment when she'd unzipped her onesie to see *that rash*.

If Olivia had lived—if meningitis had not got its sneaky grasp on her beautiful, precious child—then she would have been nine years old now. In junior school. There'd be school pictures on the mantel. Pictures that showed progress. Life. But her pictures had been frozen in time. There would be no more pictures of Olivia appearing on the walls. No more videos on her phone. No paintings on her fridge.

And I could have prevented it all if only I'd paid more attention. Alastair was right. It was all my fault.

Sydney put down her mug and hugged her knees. The anniversary of Olivia's death was getting closer. It was a day she dreaded, that relentlessly came round every year, torturing her with thoughts of what she might have done differently. Tonight she would not be able to sleep. At all.

I can't just sit here and go through that insomnia again!

She got up off the couch and looked about her for something to do. Maybe declutter a cupboard or something? Deep-clean the kitchen? Go through her books and choose some for the bookstall at the Christmas market? Something... Anything but sit there and dwell on *what ifs*!

The doorbell rang, interrupting her agonising.

She froze, then felt a rush of relief.

Thank goodness! I don't care who you are, but I'm going to talk to you. Anything to get my mind off where it's going!

She opened the door.

Nathan!

'Oh. Hi.' She'd never expected him to turn up at her door. How did he know where she lived?

Nathan looked a little uncomfortable. Uncertain. 'I...er...apologise for just turning up at your house like this.'

'Is it Lottie?'

He shook his head and scratched at his chin, looking up and down the road. 'No. I've...er... got a call-out. Nothing urgent, but...'

She'd thought that what he'd said previously about calling in on her had been a joke. Had he actually meant it?

Spending more time with the delicious Nathan since that kiss on her cheek had seemed a bad idea. She'd made a firm decision to avoid him. And now here he was!

As if in answer to her unspoken question he looked sheepish as he said, 'I looked up your home address at work. Sorry. It's just...I tried to use my GPS, but it hasn't been updated for a while and it led me to a field, so...I need your help.'

He needed to find an address! She *had* offered to help him with that, and though she'd told herself—harshly—not to spend time alone with Nathan Jones again, she was now reconsidering it. After hours of feeling herself being pulled down a dark tunnel towards all those thoughts that tortured her on a nightly basis—well, right now she welcomed his interruption. What else would she be doing anyway?

Not sleeping. That was what. The damn pills he'd given her just didn't seem to be having the desired effect. Were they different from last year's? She couldn't remember.

Nathan though was the king of light and fluffy, and that was what she needed. Plus it would be interesting to see what he did at work. And she would be helping by telling him the way to go. Anything was better than sitting in this house for another night, staring at the walls, waiting for sleep to claim her.

'Sure. I'll just get my keys.'

She tried not to be amused by the look of shock on his face when she agreed. Instead she just grabbed her coat, locked up and headed out to his car—a beat-up four-wheel drive that, quite frankly, looked as if it deserved to be in a wrecker's yard. There were dents, one panel of the car was a completely different colour from the rest of it, and where it wasn't covered in rust it was covered in mud. Even the number-plate was half hanging off, looking as if it wanted to escape.

She looked at the vehicle uncertainly. 'Does that actually work?'

He smiled fondly at it. 'She's old, but she always starts. I promise it's clean on the inside.' He rubbed the back of his neck.

Sydney almost laughed. 'Don't worry. I've got a matching one over there.' She pointed at her own vehicle and saw him notice the dried sprays of mud—not just up the bodywork, but over the back windows too.

He smiled, relaxing a little. 'That makes me feel much better.'

Sydney smiled and got into his car. 'Where are we going?'

'Long Wood Road?'

She nodded. 'I know it. It's a couple of miles from here. Take this road out of the village and when you get to the junction at the end turn right.'

'Thanks.' He gunned the engine and began to drive.

Strangely, she felt lighter. More in control. And it felt great not to be sitting in her cottage, staring at those pictures.

'Who are you going to see?'

'Eleanor Briggs?'

'I know her. She has a Russian Blue cat called Misty.'

'I'm not seeing her about Misty. I'm afraid I can't say why. Patient confidentiality prohibits me sharing that with you.'

'That's okay.' She smiled as he began heading to the outskirts of Silverdale.

It felt good next to him. Comfortable. Was that because this was business? And because he was working?

The focus isn't on me. Or us. This is just one professional helping out another.

She'd never been comfortable with being the focus of people's attention. Even as a child she'd tried to hide when she was in the school choir, or a school play. Trying her hardest not to be given a main role, trying not to be noticed. At university, when she'd had to give a solo presentation on the dangers of diabetes in dogs, she'd almost passed out from having to stand at the front of the lecture hall and present to her lecturers and tutor. The *pressure!*

But here they were, stuck in a car together,

music on the radio, and she was much more re-laxed. This was much better than being stuck at home, staring at old pictures that broke her heart.

Glancing at him driving, she noticed he'd rolled up his sleeves and that his forearms were lightly tanned, and filled with muscle as he changed gear. A chunky sports watch enveloped his wrist. He had good arms. *Attractive* arms. She glanced away.

A song came on that she knew and quietly she began singing and bobbing her head to the music.

Nathan looked over at her. 'You like this?'

Sydney nodded and he turned up the sound. She began to sing louder as it got to the chorus, laughing suddenly as Nathan joined in. Out of tune and clearly tone deaf.

They began to drive down a country road.

Silverdale was Sydney's whole life. A small pocket of English countryside that she felt was all hers. The place where she'd hoped to raise her daughter. In its community atmosphere where everyone looked out for one another.

Pushing the thought to one side, she turned back to Nathan. He was concentrating on the road now that the song was over and the DJ was babbling, his brow slightly furrowed, both hands gripping the wheel.

'You need to take the next left. Long Woods Road.'

Nathan indicated, following the twists and turns of her directions, and soon she was pointing out Eleanor's small cottage. They turned into the driveway and parked in front of the house. Killing the engine, he turned to her. 'Thank you. I wouldn't have got here without you.'

'And I wouldn't have had my eardrums assaulted.'

He raised an eyebrow.

'Your singing.'

'I have a lovely voice. I'll have you know that when I was in my school choir I was the only child not selected to sing a solo.'

She smirked. 'You should be proud.'

'I am.'

Then he grinned and reached for his bag, which was down by her feet. She moved slightly, out of his way, as he lifted it up and past her.

He was smiling still. Looking at her. She

watched as his gaze dropped to her mouth and instantly the atmosphere changed.

Sydney looked away, pretending that something out of the window had caught her eye.

'Will you be okay for a while? I can leave the radio on.'

She didn't look at him, but dug her phone from her pocket. 'I've got my phone. I'm playing a word game against my veterinary nurse.'

Nathan said nothing, but got out of the car. Once he was gone, she suddenly felt *alone*. His presence had filled the car, and now that he was gone it seemed so empty. The only reminder a very faint aroma of cologne. She would never have thought that spending time with Nathan would be so easy, after their coffee together. But he'd been just what she needed tonight. Bad singing included.

In the sky above stars were beginning to filter through the dark, twinkling and shining. She looked for the biggest and brightest. Olivia's star. The one she had once pointed out to her daughter as her very own special light. Just remembering that night with her daughter made her eyes sting with unshed tears, but she blinked them away.

I can't keep crying. I've got to be stronger than this!

She switched on her phone and stared at the game she no longer wanted to play.

It was pitch-black along the country roads as they followed behind another four-wheel drive that was towing a horsebox. In the back, Sydney could see a large black horse, easily fifteen hands high. Was it the Daltons? They had a horse like that. Though she guessed it could be the Webbers' horse. They had one like it too. Or maybe it wasn't anyone she knew. She didn't get called out to *all* the horses in the Silverdale area. There was a specialised equine veterinary service in Norton Town. Sometimes she worked alongside it.

As they drove back along Long Wood Road, Sydney realised she was feeling more relaxed and happy than she had for a few weeks. It was strange. Perhaps it was a good thing not to be wallowing in her memories tonight. Perhaps getting out and about and doing something was the right thing to do.

I need a hobby. An evening class. Something. Maybe it'll be better when we start those meetings for the Christmas market and fête.

What she knew for sure was that she had felt better when she'd seen Nathan returning to the car. Seen his smile. Felt his warmth. Knowing that he wasn't the type to pry into her past. He made her feel weirdly comfortable, despite the physical response she felt. It was something she hadn't felt for a long time, and she was really glad she'd agreed to come out with him and spend some more time with him.

She was just about to say something about it—thank him for earlier—when she spotted something, off to Nathan's right, illuminated by the lights of the vehicles. It was a small herd of deer, running across the field at full pelt.

'Nathan, look!' She pointed.

There had to be seven or eight. Mostly fully grown and running hard. The lead deer had full antlers, like tree branches.

And they were heading straight for the road.

'I think I'm going to slow down.'

But as Nathan slowed their vehicle it became clear that the vehicle in front, with the horse trailer, had continued on at a normal speed.

Sydney leaned forward. 'Have they not seen them? What can we do?'

Nathan hit his horn, hoping it would make the driver ahead pay attention, or at least startle the deer into heading in another direction, but neither happened.

The biggest deer burst through the undergrowth, leaping over the ditch and straight out onto the road—right in front of the other vehicle.

Sydney watched, horrified, and brake lights lit up her face as the car in front tried to swerve at the last minute, but failed. The horsebox at the back wobbled, bouncing from left to right with the weight of the horse inside, before it tipped over and pulled the car straight into the ditch. The rest of the deer leapt by, over the road and into the next field.

Nathan hit the brakes, stopping the car. 'Call for help.'

Her heart was pounding madly in her chest. 'What are you going to do?'

'I'm going to check for casualties. After you've contacted emergency services go into the boot of the car and find the reflective triangle and put it in the road. We're on a bend here, and we need to warn other traffic. We're sitting ducks.'

Then he grabbed his bag and was gone.

She watched him run over to the car through the light of the headlamps as she dialled 999 with shaking fingers. As she watched Nathan trying to talk to someone she saw the driver fall from the driver's side. Then her gaze fell upon the horse in the horsebox. It was moving. Alive.

I have to get out there!

But she had no equipment. No bag. No medicines. She felt helpless. Useless! She'd felt this way just once before.

I'll be damned if I feel that way again!

'Which service do you require?' A voice spoke down the phone.

'*All of them*. We need them all.'

CHAPTER FOUR

SYDNEY DASHED TO the boot of Nathan's car and panicked as she struggled to open it. At first she couldn't see the reflective triangle he'd mentioned—his boot was full of *stuff.* But she rummaged through, tossing things to one side, until she found it. Then she dashed to the bend in the road and placed it down, hoping that it would be enough of a warning to stop any other vehicles that came that way from running into them.

She ran over to the ditched car and horsebox, glancing quickly at the horse in the back. It was neighing and huffing, making an awful lot of noise, stamping its hooves, struggling to find a way to stand in a box that was on its side. She couldn't see if it had any injuries. She hoped not. But there wasn't much she could do for the horse anyhow. She needed to help Nathan and the people in the car.

She'd already seen the driver was out of the vehicle. He was sitting in the road, groaning and clutching at his head. He had a bleeding laceration across his brow, causing blood to dribble down his face and eyes.

Nathan was in the ditched vehicle, assessing whoever was in the front seat.

Sydney knelt down, saw the head wound was quite deep and pulled the scarf from around her neck and tied it around the guy's scalp. 'You need to come with me. Off the road. Come and sit over here.'

She pointed at the grass verge.

'I didn't see...I didn't notice... We were arguing...' the man mumbled.

He was in shock. Sydney grabbed the man under his armpits and hauled him to his feet. Normally she wouldn't move anyone after a car accident. She knew that much. But this man had already hauled himself out of the vehicle and dropped onto the road before Nathan got there. If he'd done any damage to himself, then it was already done. The least she could do was get him out of the middle of the road and to a safer zone.

The man was heavy and dazed, but he got to his feet and staggered with her to the roadside, where she lowered him down and told him to stay. 'Don't move. Try and stay still until the ambulance gets here. I've called for help—they're on their way.'

The man looked up at her. 'My wife...*my son*!'

He tried to get up again, but Sydney held him firmly in place. 'I'll go and help them, but you *must* stay here!'

The man looked helpless and nodded, trembling as he realised there was blood all over his hands.

Sydney ran back over to the ditched car, heard a child crying and noticed that Nathan was now in the back seat. He called to her over his shoulder.

'There's a baby. In a car seat. He looks okay, but I need to get him out of the vehicle so I can sit in the back and maintain C-spine for the mother.'

Sydney nodded and glanced at the woman in the front seat. She was unconscious, and her air bag had deployed and lay crumpled and used before her. There was no bleeding that she could see, but that didn't mean a serious injury had not occurred. If a casualty was unconscious, that usually meant shock or a head injury. She hoped it was just the former.

'I'm unclipping the seatbelt.'

Sydney heard a clunk, then Nathan was backing out, holding a car seat with an indignant, crying infant inside it, bawling away.

The baby couldn't be more than nine months old, and had beautiful fluffy blond hair. But his face was red with rage and tears, and his little feet in his sleep suit were kicking in time with his crying.

'Shh… It's okay. It's okay…I've got you.' Sydney took the heavy seat with care, cooing calming words as she walked back across the road to take him to his father.

In the distance she heard the faint, reassuring sound of sirens.

'Here. Your little boy. What's his name?' she asked the man, who smiled with great relief that his son seemed physically okay.

'Brandon.'

That was good. The man's bump to the head hadn't caused amnesia or anything like that. 'And your name…?'

'Paul.'

'Okay, Paul. You're safe. And Brandon's safe—he doesn't look injured—and that man helping your wife is a doctor. She's in good hands. He knows what he's doing.'

'Is she hurt? Is Helen hurt?'

Sydney debated about how much she should reveal—should she say that Helen was unconscious? Or stay optimistic and just tell him she was doing okay? The truth won out.

'I don't know. She's unconscious, but Nathan—that's Dr Jones—is with her in the car and he's looking after her. Do you hear those sirens? More help will be with us soon.'

The sirens were much louder now, and Sydney knew she was breathing faster. Hearing them get closer and closer just reminded her of that morning when she'd had to call an ambulance for Olivia. Wishing they'd get to her faster. Feeling that they were taking for ever. Praying that they would help her daughter. She could see the same look in Paul's eyes now. The distress. The *fear.*

But this was an occasion where she actually had her wits about her and could do something.

'I need to go and help Nathan.'

She ran back across the road. The car's radiator or something must have burst, because she could hear hissing and see steam rising up through the bonnet of the vehicle. She ducked into the open door.

Nathan was in the back seat, his hands clutching Helen's head, keeping it upright and still. His face was twisted, as if *he* was in pain.

'Is she breathing still?' he managed to ask her.

Is she *breathing?* Sydney wasn't sure she wanted to check—her own shock at what had happened was starting to take effect. What if Helen wasn't breathing? What if Helen's heart had stopped?

'I—'

'Watch her chest. Is there rise and fall?'

She checked. There was movement. 'Yes, there is!'

'Count how many breaths she takes in ten seconds.'

She looked back, counting. 'Two.'

'Okay. That's good.'

She saw Nathan wince. Perhaps he had cramp, or something? There was some broken glass in the car. Perhaps he'd knelt on it? She pushed the thought to the back of her mind as vehicles flashing red and blue lights appeared. An ambulance. A fire engine, and further behind them she could see a police car.

Thank you!

Sydney got out of the car and waved them down, feeling relief flood her.

A paramedic jumped out of the ambulance and came over to her, pulling on some purple gloves. 'Can you tell me what happened?'

She gave a brief rundown of the incident, and pointed out Paul and baby Brandon, then filled him in on the woman in the car.

'Okay, let's see to her first.' The paramedic called out to his partner to look after the driver and his son whilst he checked out Helen, still in the car with Nathan.

Sydney ran back over to Paul. 'Help's here! It's okay. We're okay.' She beamed, glad that the onus of responsibility was now being shouldered by lots of other people rather than just her and Nathan.

As she stood back and watched the rescue operation she realised there were tears on her face. She wiped them away with a sleeve, aware of how frightened she'd been, and waited for Nathan to join her, shivering. She wanted to be held. To feel safe. She wanted to be comforted.

The morning she'd found Olivia she'd been on her own. Alastair had already left for work. So there'd been no one to hold her and let her know it was okay. She'd needed arms around her then and she needed them now. But Alastair had never held her again.

If she asked him, Nathan would hold her for a moment. She just knew it. Sensed it. What they'd just experienced had been traumatic. But she remained silent, clutching her coat to her. She just stood and watched the emergency services get everything sorted.

And waited.

Nathan was needed by the paramedics, and then by the police, and by the time he was free she was not. The horse needed her—needed checking over.

She told herself a hug wasn't important and focused on the practical.

Paul and Brandon had been taken to hospital in one ambulance; Helen had been extricated and taken away in another, finally conscious. The horsebox had been righted and the horse had been led out to be checked by Sydney. It had some knocks and scrapes to its legs, mostly around its fetlocks—which, in humans, was comparable to injuries to an ankle joint—but apart from that it just seemed startled more than anything.

They'd all been very lucky, and Sydney now stood, calming the horse, whilst they waited for an animal transporter to arrive.

Nathan stood watching her. 'That horse really feels safe with you.'

She smiled. 'Makes a change. Normally horses see me coming with my vet bag and start playing up. It's nice to be able to comfort one and calm it down.'

'You're doing brilliantly.'

She looked at him. He looked a little worn out. Wearied. As if attending to the patients in the crash had physically exhausted him. Perhaps he'd had a really long day. Just like being a vet, being a doctor had to be stressful at times. Seeing endless streams of people, each with their own problems. Having to break bad news. She knew how stressful it was for her to have to tell a customer that their beloved pet was dying, or had to be put to sleep. And when she *did* euthanise a beloved pet she often found herself shedding silent tears along with the owner. She couldn't help it.

Perhaps it was the same for Nathan. Did seeing people in distress upset him? Wear him out?

'*You* did brilliantly. Knowing what to do...who to treat. How to look after Helen. I wouldn't have thought to do that.' She stroked the horse's muzzle.

'It's nothing.'

'But it is. You probably saved her life, keeping her airway open like that. She could have died.'

'At least they're in safe hands now.'

She looked at him and met his gaze. 'They were *already* in safe hands.'

She needed to let him know that what he'd done today had *mattered*. Paul still had a wife. Brandon still had a mother. Because of *him*. A while ago she'd almost lost her faith in doctors. She'd depended on them to save Olivia, and when they'd told her there was nothing they could do...

At first she hadn't wanted to believe them. Had *raged* at them. Demanded they do *something*! When they hadn't she had collapsed in a heap, hating them—and everyone—with a passion she had never known was inside her. Today, Nathan had proved to her that doctors did help.

'How do you think the horse is doing?'

Sydney could feel the animal was calmer. It had stopped stamping its hooves and snorting as they'd stood there on the side of the road, watching the clean-up operation. It had stopped tossing its head. Its breathing had become steadier.

'She's doing great.'

'Paul and Helen aren't the only ones in safe hands.' He smiled and sat down on the bank beside her, letting out a breath and rolling his shoulders.

She stared at him for a moment, shocked to realise that she wanted to sit next to him, maybe to massage his shoulders or just lean her head against his shoulder. She wanted that physical contact.

Feeling that yearning to touch him surprised her and she turned away from him, focussing on the horse. She shouldn't be feeling that for him. What was the point? It was best to focus on the horse. She knew what she was doing there.

It didn't take long for the accident to be cleared. The police took pictures, measured the road, measured the skid marks and collected debris. The car was pulled from the ditch and lifted onto a lorry to be taken away, and just as Sydney was beginning to doubt that a new horsebox would ever arrive a truck came ambling around the corner and they loaded the mare onto it to take her back to her stable.

Sydney gave the truck driver her details and told her to let Paul know that she'd be happy to come out and check on the horse, and that he was to give her a call if she was needed urgently.

Eventually she and Nathan got back into his car and she noticed that it was nearly midnight. Normally she would be lying in bed at this time, staring at the ceiling and worrying over every little thought. Wide awake.

But tonight she felt tired. Ready for her bed even without a sleeping pill. It surprised her.

Nathan started the engine. 'Let's take you home. Our little trip out lasted longer than either of us expected.'

'That's okay. I'd only have been awake anyway. At least this way I was put to good use.'

'You've not been sleeping for some time?'

She shook her head and looked away from him, out of the window. 'No.'

He seemed to ruminate on this for a while, but then he changed the subject. 'Good thing I didn't get any more house calls.'

That was true. What would he have done if he'd got a page to say that someone was having chest pains whilst he'd been helping Helen? They'd been lucky. All of them.

It was nice and warm in Nathan's car as he drove them steadily back to Silverdale. For the first time Sydney felt the silence between them was comfortable. She didn't need to fill the silence with words. Or to feel awkward. The circumstances of the emergency had thrown them together and something intangible had changed.

It felt nice to be sitting with someone like that. Even if it *was* with a man she had at first disliked immensely.

A jolt in the road startled her, and she realised she'd almost nodded off. She sucked in a breath, shocked that she'd felt comfortable enough to fall asleep.

She glanced at Nathan just as he glanced at her, and they both quickly looked away.

Sydney smiled.

It was beginning to feel more than nice.

It was beginning to feel *good*.

Nathan pulled up outside Sydney's cottage and killed the engine. He looked out at the dark, empty street, lit only by one or two streetlamps, and watched as a cat sneaked across the road and disappeared under a hedge after being startled by his engine.

Despite the accident he'd had a good time tonight. It had felt really good to spend time with Sydney, and he felt they'd cleared the air after their misunderstandings at their first meeting and the awkward coffee.

Turning up at her door to ask for help with directions had almost been a step too far for him. He'd joked about asking her for her help, but when he'd tried to find Eleanor's cottage on his own his stupid GPS had made him turn down a very narrow farming lane and asked him to drive through a muddy field! He'd got out and checked that there wasn't a farmhouse or something near, where he might ask for help, but there'd been nothing. Just fields. And mud. Plenty of mud!

He'd argued with himself about going to her house. Almost not gone there at all. He knew her address. He'd seen it on his computer at work and for some reason it had burnt itself into his brain. She didn't live far from her place of work, so it had been easy to find her, but he hadn't known what sort of reception he'd get. She might have slammed the door in his face.

He'd felt awkward asking for help, but thankfully she'd agreed to go with him, and it had been nice to have her with him in his car, just chatting. It had been a very long time since he'd done that with anyone. The last time had been with Gwyneth. She'd always talked when they were driving—pointing things out, forming opinions on people or places that they passed. Her judgemental approach had made him realise just how insecure she'd been, and he'd done his best to try and make her feel good about herself.

Tonight, Sydney had been invaluable at the accident site—something he knew Gwyneth would never have been. She'd not been great with blood.

Sydney had been brilliant, looking after the driver and the baby, and then she'd managed to calm the horse and check it over. He wouldn't have known how to handle such a large animal. He barely coped with looking after a rabbit, never mind a terrified horse that had been thrown around in a tin box.

Now they were back to that moment again. The

one where he normally kissed people goodbye. And suddenly there was that tension again. He wasn't sure whether he should lean over and just do it. Just kiss her.

'Thanks for everything tonight. I couldn't have done it without you,' he said honestly.

She'd grabbed her handbag from the footwell on her side and sat with it on her knee. 'No problem. I couldn't have done it without you either.'

Though half her face was in shadow, he could still see her smile.

'Well…goodnight, Sydney.'

'Goodnight, Nathan.'

She stared at him for a moment, and then turned away and grabbed the latch to open the door. It wouldn't budge and she struggled with it for a moment or two.

'Sorry…sometimes it catches.'

He leant over her for the handle and she flinched as he reached past her and undid the door for her. He sat back, worried that he'd made her start.

She hurried from the vehicle without saying a word, throwing the strap of her bag over her shoulder and delving into her coat pocket for her house keys.

Disappointment filled his soul. He didn't want her to walk away feeling awkward. That flinch, it had been... He wanted...

What do I want?

'Sydney?' He was out of his car before he could even think about what he was doing. He stood there, looking over the top of his car, surprising even himself. The night air had turned chill and he could feel goosebumps trembling up his spine.

She'd turned, curious. 'Yes?'

'Um...' He couldn't think of anything to say! What was he even doing, anyway? He couldn't turn this friendship with Sydney into anything more. Neither of them was ready for that. And there was Anna to think of too. He was sure Sydney would not want to take on someone with a little girl—not after losing her own. And surely she wouldn't want to take on someone who was ill?

Gwyneth had made it quite clear that he wasn't worth *her* time and affection. That he had somehow ruined her life with his presence. Did he want to put someone else through that? Someone like Sydney? Who'd already been through so much? He'd end up needing her more than she needed him, and he'd hate that imbalance. He knew the state of his health. His condition would make him a burden. And Anna had to be his top priority. And yet...

And yet something about her *pulled* at him. Her energy. Her presence. Those grey eyes that looked so studious and wise, yet at the same time contained a hurt and a loss that even he couldn't fully understand. He'd lost his fiancée, yes, but that had been through separation. It wasn't the same as losing a child. Nowhere near it. He and Gwyneth had hardly been the love story of the century.

Even though he'd only known Sydney for a couple of days, there was something in her nature that...

'Remember to take your sleeping pill.'

Remember to take your sleeping pill? Really? That's what you come up with?

Her face filled with relief. 'Oh. Yes, I will. Thank you.'

Relief. *See?* She was being polite. She was probably desperate to get inside and away from him, because he clearly had no idea how to talk to women, having spent the last few years of his life just being a father and—

Being a father is more important than your ability to chat up women!

'You get a good night's sleep yourself. You've earned it.'

He opened his mouth to utter a reply, but she'd already slipped her key into the lock. She raised her hand in a brief goodbye and then was inside, her door closing with a shocking finality, and he was left standing in the street, staring at a closed door.

Nathan watched as Sydney switched on the lights. He ducked inside his car as she came to her window and closed the curtains. He stared for a few minutes, then tore his gaze away, worried about what her neighbours might think. He started the engine, turned up the heater and slowly drove away. Berating himself for not saying something more inspiring, something witty—something that would have had her...*what?*

That wasn't who he was. Those clever, witty guys, who always had the perfect line for every occasion, lived elsewhere. He didn't have a script-writer to think up clever things for him to say that would charm her and make her like him more. He wasn't suave, or sophisticated, or one of those charming types who could have women at their beck and call with a click of their fingers.

And he didn't *want* to be a man like that. He was a single dad, with a gorgeous, clever daughter who anyone would be lucky to know. He led an uncomplicated life. He worked hard.

What did he want to achieve with Sydney? And why was he getting involved anyway? His own fiancée—the woman he'd been willing to pledge his entire life to—had walked away from him, and if someone who'd once said they loved him could do that, then a relative stranger like Sydney might do the same thing. She didn't strike him as someone looking to settle down again, to start a relationship in a ready-made family. Especially not with another little girl after losing her own.

Did she?

No.

So why on earth could he not get her out of his head?

* * *

Nathan was fighting fatigue. Over the last few days he'd been having a small relapse in his symptoms, and he'd been suffering with painful muscle spasms, cramps, and an overwhelming tiredness that just wouldn't go away. That accident had aggravated it. It was probably stress.

As he downed some painkillers he knew he'd have to hide his discomfort from his daughter. She mustn't see him weaken. Not yet. It was still early days. He didn't want her to suspect that there was something wrong. He had to keep going for her. Had to keep being strong. Normally he could hide it. And he needed his energy for today. Anna was still too young to understand about his condition. How did you explain multiple sclerosis to a six-year-old?

Today Lottie was due for her next check-up, and he was feeling some anticipation at seeing Sydney. At work, during breaks, he often found himself itching to cross the road on some pretext, just to see if she was there, but for the life of him he couldn't think of anything to say. His inner critic kept reminding him that seeing her was probably a bad idea. The woman practically had 'Keep Out' signs hanging around her neck, and she'd certainly not divulged anything too personal to him. She hadn't even mentioned her daughter to him.

And yet…

'Anna! Come on, it's time to go.'

'Are we taking Lottie now?'

'We are. But we're walking because…' he reached for a plausible excuse '…it's a nice day.' He smiled, reaching out for the counter as a small wave of dizziness affected his balance briefly. Of all his symptoms, dizziness and feeling off-balance were the worst. He couldn't drive like this. It would be dangerous. And at least the crisp, fresh winter air would make him feel better.

'Yay!' Anna skipped off to fetch Lottie's carrier.

He managed to stop the world spinning and stood up straight, sucking in a deep breath.

The rabbit was doing quite well, Nathan thought. She was eating and drinking as normal, had come off the medication and was settled back outside. The bite wounds had healed cleanly and

Lottie's eye had escaped surgery, much to both his and Anna's delight. They were hopeful for a full recovery.

With Lottie in her box, Nathan locked up and they headed to the veterinary practice. He still wasn't feeling great—quite tired and light-headed—but he tried to keep up a level of bright chatter as they walked along the village roads.

His daughter hopped alongside him, pointing out robins and magpies and on one particular occasion a rather large snail.

The walk took a while. They lived a good couple of miles from the practice and his arms ached from carrying Lottie, who seemed to get weightier with every step, but eventually they got there, and Nathan settled into a waiting room seat with much relief.

He didn't get to enjoy it for too long, though.

Sydney had opened her door. 'Do you want to bring Lottie in?'

Sydney looked well, though there were still faint dark circles beneath her eyes. It felt good to see her again. He carried Lottie through and put her onto the examination table.

'How's she doing?'

He nodded, but that upset his balance and he had to grip the examination table to centre himself.

Had Sydney noticed?

He swallowed, suppressing his nausea. 'Er... good. Eating and drinking. The eye's clean and she seems okay.' He decided to focus on Sydney's face. When he got dizzy like this it helped to focus on something close to him. She wasn't moving that much, and he needed a steady point to remain fixed on.

'Let's take a look.'

Sydney frowned, concern etched across her normally soft features as she concentrated on the examination. She was very thorough, reminding him of her capability and passion. She checked Lottie's eye, her bite wounds, her temperature and gave her a thorough going-over.

'I agree with you. She seems to have recovered well. I think we can discharge this patient.' She stood up straight again and smiled.

'That's great.'

He realised she was looking at him questioningly.

'Are you okay?'

Nathan felt another wave of nausea sweep over him as dizziness assailed him again. 'Er...not really...'

Had the walk been too much? Was he dehydrated?

Sydney glanced at Anna uncertainly, then came around the desk and took Nathan's arm and guided him over to a small stool in the corner. 'I'll get you some water.'

He sank his head into his hands as the dizziness passed, and was just starting to feel it clear a bit when she returned with a glass. He tried not to look at Anna until he was sure he could send her a reassuring smile to say everything was okay.

He took a sip of the drink. 'Thanks.'

'Missed breakfast?'

He gratefully accepted the excuse. 'Yes. Yes, I did. Must have got a bit light-headed, that's all.'

'Daddy, you had toast with jam for breakfast.' Anna contradicted.

He smiled. 'But not enough, obviously.'

'You had three slices.'

He smiled at his daughter, who was blowing his cover story quite innocently. He was afraid to look at Sydney, but she was making sure Lottie was secure in her cage.

Then she turned to look at him, staring intently, her brow lined. 'Are you safe to get home, Dr Jones?'

He stood up. 'We walked here. And I'm fine.' He didn't want to let her see how ill he felt.

'You don't look it. You look very pale.'

'Right...' He glanced at Anna. 'Perhaps I just need some more fresh air.' He took another sip of water.

Sydney stood in front of him, arms crossed. 'You don't seem in a fit state to walk home yet. Or to take care of Anna.'

'I am!' he protested.

'You had nystagmus. I know your world is spinning.'

Nystagmus was a rapid movement of the eyes in response to the semi-circular canals being stimulated. In effect, if the balance centre told you your world was spinning, your eyes tried to play catch-up in order to focus.

'Look, let me tell my next client I'll be ten minutes and I'll drive you both back.'

'No—no, it's fine! I can't disrupt your workday, that's ridiculous. I'm okay now. Besides, that would annoy your patient. I'm fine.'

He stood up to prove it, but swayed slightly, and she had to reach for him, grabbing his waist to steady him.

'Honestly. I just need to get some air for a moment. I could go and sit down across the road at the surgery, maybe. Check my blood pressure. Have a cup of sweet tea. It'll pass—it always does.' He smiled broadly, to show her he was feeling better, even though he wasn't.

She let go of him. 'You're sure?'

No.

'Absolutely.'

He saw her face fill with doubt and hesitation. 'Maybe Anna could stay here with me. She could look after the animals in the back. Give them cuddles, or something.'

Anna gasped, her smile broad. '*Could* I, Daddy?'

He didn't want to impose on Sydney. He could see it had been tough for her to offer that, and she was working. Anna should be *his* responsibility, not someone else's.

'Er... I don't know, honey. Sydney's very busy.'

'It's no problem. Olivia used to do it all the time.' She blushed and looked away.

Her daughter.

'Are you sure?'

'I'm sure. You're clearly unwell today. She can stay with me for the day and I'll drive you both home when I finish. Around four.'

Anna was jumping up and down with joy, clapping her hands together in absolute glee at this amazing turn of events.

He really didn't want to do this, but what choice did he have? Sydney was right. And hadn't he wanted to move to a village to experience this very support?

'Fine. Thank you.' He knelt to speak to his excited daughter. 'You be good for Sydney. Do what you're told and behave—yes?'

She nodded.

Standing up, he felt a little head rush. Maybe Sydney was right. Perhaps he *did* need a break.

He was just having a difficult time letting someone help him. It irked him, gnawing away at him like a particularly persistent rodent. How could he look after his daughter if he was going to let a little dizziness affect him? And this was just the *start* of his condition. These were mild symptoms. It would get worse. And already he was relying on other people to look after his daughter—Sydney, of all people!

'Perhaps she ought to stay with—'

Sydney grabbed his arm and started to guide him towards her exit. 'Go and lie down, Dr Jones.'

Nathan grimaced hard, then kissed the top of his daughter's head and left.

It had been a delight to have Anna with her for the day. The invitation to look after Nathan's little girl had just popped out. She'd not carefully considered exactly what it would mean to look after the little girl before she'd said it, and once she had she'd felt a small amount of alarm at her offer.

But Anna had been wonderful. She was sweet, calm with the animals, with a natural affection and understanding of them that those in her care gravitated towards, allowing her to stroke them. The cats had purred. Dogs had wagged their tails or showed their bellies to be rubbed. And Anna had asked loads of questions about them, showing a real interest. She'd even told Sydney that she wanted to be a vet when she was older! That had been sweet.

Olivia had liked being with the animals, but she'd only liked the cuddling part. The oohing and aahing over cute, furry faces. Anna was different. She wanted to know what breed they were. What they were at the vet's for. How Sydney might make them better. It had been good to share her knowledge with Nathan's daughter. Good to see the differences between the two little girls.

Once they were done for the day, and the last of the records had been completed, she smiled as Lucy complained about her sore back after cleaning cages all afternoon, but then sat down to eat not one but two chocolate bars, because she felt ravenous.

They sat together, chatting about animal care, and Anna listened quietly, not interrupting, and not getting in the way.

When she'd gathered her things, Sydney told Anna it was time to go.

'Thank you for having me, Sydney.'

She eyed the little girl holding her hand as they crossed the road to collect Nathan. 'Not a problem, Anna. It was lovely to have you. Let's hope your daddy is feeling better soon, hmm?'

'Daddy always gets sick and tired. He pretends he's not, but I know when he is.'

'Perhaps he *is* just tired? He does a very important job, looking after everyone.' But something niggled at her. The way Nathan had been, and the nonchalant way Anna had mentioned that *'Daddy always gets sick and tired...'*

Was Nathan ill? And, if so, what could it be? Just a virus? Was he generally run-down? Or could it be something else? Something serious?

They quickly crossed to the surgery and collected a rather pale-looking Nathan. He insisted he was feeling much better. Suspecting he wasn't quite being truthful, she got him into the car and started the engine, glancing at Anna on the back seat through the rearview mirror.

Anna smiled, and the sight went straight to Sydney's heart. To distract herself, she rummaged in the glovebox to see if she had any of Olivia's old CDs. She found one and slid it into the CD player, and soon they were singing along with a cartoon meerkat and a warthog.

Driving through the village, she found herself smiling, amazed that she still remembered the words, and laughing at Anna singing in the back. It felt *great* to be driving along, singing together. She and Olivia had always used to do it. It was even putting a smile on Nathan's face.

Much too soon she found herself at Nathan's house, and she walked them both up to their front door, finally handing them Lottie's carrier.

Nathan smiled broadly. 'Thanks, Sydney. I really appreciate it. I got a lot of rest and I feel much better.'

'Glad to hear it. Anna was brilliant. The animals adored her.'

'They all do. Thanks again.'

'No problem. See you around.'

She began to walk away, turning to give a half wave, feeling embarrassed at doing so. She got in her car and drove away as fast as she could—before she was tempted to linger and revel in the feeling of family once again.

It felt odd to be back in the car, alone again after that short while she'd been with Anna and Nathan. The car seemed empty. The music had been silenced and returned to the glovebox.

By the time she got home her heart physically ached.

And she sat in her daughter's old room for a very long time, just staring at the empty walls.

CHAPTER FIVE

SOMEHOW IT HAD become December, and November had passed in a moment. A moment when natural sleep had continued to elude her, but her strange, mixed feelings for the new village doctor had not.

She'd listened as her own clients had chatted with her about the new doctor, smiled when they'd joked about how gorgeous he was, how heroic he was. Had she heard that he'd saved lives already? One woman in the village, who really ought to have known better, had even joked and blushed about Dr Jones giving her the kiss of life! Sydney had smiled politely, but inside her heart had been thundering.

She'd seen him fleetingly, here and there. A couple of times he'd waved at her. Once she'd bumped into him in the sandwich shop, just as a large dollop of coleslaw had squeezed itself from her crusty cob and splatted onto her top.

'Oh!' He'd laughed, rummaging in his pockets and pulling out a fresh white handkerchief. 'Here—take this.'

She'd blushed madly, accepted his hankie, and then had stood there wiping furiously at her clothes, knowing that he was standing there, staring at her. When she'd looked up to thank him *he'd* blushed, and she'd wondered what he had been thinking about.

Then they'd both gone on their way, and she'd looked over her shoulder at him at the exact moment when he'd done the same.

She felt that strange undercurrent whenever they met, or whenever she saw him. She kept trying to ignore it. Trying to ignore *him*. But it was difficult. Her head and her heart had differing reactions. Her head told her to stay away and keep her distance. But her heart and her body sang whenever he was near, as if it was saying, *Look, there he is! Give him a wave! Go and say hello! Touch him!*

Today frost covered the ground like a smattering of icing sugar, and the village itself looked very picturesque. Sydney was desperate to get out and go for a walk around the old bridleways, maybe take a few pictures with her camera, but she couldn't. There was far too much to do and she was running late for a committee meeting.

The Silverdale Christmas market and nativity was an annual festive occasion that was always held the week before Christmas. People came from all around the county, sometimes further from afield, and it was a huge financial boost to local businesses during the typically slower winter months. Unfortunately this year it was scheduled to fall on the one day that she dreaded. The anniversary of Olivia's death.

Sydney had previously been one of the organisers, but after what had happened with Olivia she hadn't been involved much. Barely at all. This year she'd decided to get back into it. She'd always been needed, especially where the animals were concerned. She'd used to judge the Best Pet show, and maintain the welfare of all the animals that got involved in the very real nativity—

donkeys, sheep, cows, goats, even chickens and geese! But she'd also been in charge of the flower stalls and the food market.

It was a huge commitment, but one she had enjoyed in the past. And this year it would keep her busy. Would stop her thinking of another Christmas without her daughter. Stop her from wallowing in the fact that, yet again, she would not be buying her child any gifts to put under a non-existent tree.

She sat at the table with the rest of the committee, waiting for the last member to arrive. Dr Jones was late. Considerably so. And the more they waited, the more restless she got.

'Perhaps we should just make a start and then fill Dr Jones in if he ever gets here?' Sydney suggested.

Everyone else was about to agree when the door burst open and in he came, cheeks red from the cold outside, apologising profusely. 'Sorry, everyone, I got called out to some stomach pains—which, surprisingly, turned out to be a bouncing baby boy.'

There were surprised gasps and cheers from the others.

'Who's had a baby?' asked Malcolm, the chairman.

Nathan tucked his coat over the back of his chair. 'Lucy Carter.'

Sydney sat forward, startled. '*My* Lucy Carter? My veterinary nurse?'

His gaze met hers and he beamed a smile at her which went straight to her heart. 'The very same.'

'B-but...she wasn't pregnant!' she spluttered with indignation.

'The baby in her arms would beg to differ!'

'But...'

She couldn't believe it! Okay, Lucy had put some weight on recently, but they'd put that down to those extra chocolate bars she'd been eating... *Pregnant? That's amazing!* She felt the need to go and see her straight away. To give her a hug and maybe get a cuddle with the newborn.

'It was a shock for everyone involved. But they're both doing well and everyone's happy. She told me to let you know.'

A baby. For Lucy. That was great news. And such a surprise!

It meant more work for Sydney for a bit, of course, but she'd cope. She could get an agency member of staff in. It would be weird, not seeing Lucy at work for a while. They'd always worked together. They knew each other's ways and foibles.

She sighed. Everyone else seemed to be moving on. Lucy and her new baby. Alastair and his new bride, with a baby on the way. Everyone was getting on with their lives. And she...? She was still here. In the village she's been born in. With no child. No husband. No family of her own except her elderly parents, who lived too far away anyway.

She looked across at Nathan as he settled into his seat and felt a sudden burst of irritation towards him. She'd been looking forward to getting involved in these meetings again, getting back out there into the community, and yet now her feelings towards him were making her feel uncomfortable. Was it because he'd brought news that meant her life was going to change again?

'Let's get started, shall we?' suggested Malcolm. 'First off, I'd like to welcome Dr Nathan Jones to the committee. He has taken over the role from its previous incumbent, Dr Richard Preston.'

The group clapped, smiled and nodded a welcome for their new member. Sydney stared at him, her face impassive. He looked ridiculously attractive today. Fresh-faced. Happy. She focused on his hands. Hands that had just recently delivered a baby. And she felt guilty for having allowed herself to succumb to that brief, petty jealousy. She looked up at his face and caught him looking at her, and she looked away, embarrassed.

'I'd also like to welcome Sydney back to the committee! Sydney, as I'm sure most of you know, took a little…sabbatical, if you will, from the organisation of this annual event, and I'm most pleased to have her back in full fighting form!'

She smiled as she felt all eyes turn to her, and nodded hellos to the group members she knew well and hadn't worked with for so long. It did feel good to be back here and doing something for the community again. The Christmas market and nativity was something she hadn't been able to find any pleasure in for some time, but now she was ready.

At least she hoped she was.

'The market is going to be held in the same place as always—the centre of the village square—and I believe we've already got lots of things in place from last year. Miriam?'

Miriam, the secretary, filled them in on all the recent developments. Lots of the same stalls that came every year had rebooked. Music was going to be covered by the same brass band, and the school was going to provide a choir as well.

Sydney listened, scribbling things down on her pad that she'd need to remember, and thought of past activities. There was a lot to take in—she'd forgotten how much organising there was!—and as her list got longer and longer she almost wished she could write with both hands.

She'd also forgotten how soothing these meetings could be sometimes. The hum of voices, the opinions of everyone on how things should be done, the ebb and flow of ideas… She truly appreciated the need for all this planning and preparation. Even though sometimes the older members of the committee enjoyed their dedication to picking over details a little too much.

Briefly, she allowed her mind to wander, and the memory that sprang to her mind was of a happier year, when Olivia had played the part of Mary in the nativity. In the weeks beforehand Sydney had taught her how to ride the donkey, shown her how to behave around the other animals. She remembered holding her daughter's hand as they walked through the market stalls, making sure she didn't eat too many sweets or pieces of cake, and listening to her singing carols in the choir.

She smiled, feeling a little sad. She had those memories on camera. Alastair had videoed Olivia riding the donkey in the nativity, with her fake pregnancy bump. Olivia had loved that belly, rubbing her hands over it like a real pregnant mother soothing away imaginary kicks.

'And that brings us back to our star players for the nativity,' Malcolm continued. 'I have been reliably informed by Miss Howarth of Silverdale Infants School that our Mary this year will be played by Anna Jones, and Joseph will be Barney Brooks...'

Sydney was pulled from her reverie. *Anna? Dr Jones's Anna? She was going to play Mary?* Visions flashed through her mind. Anna wearing Olivia's costume... Anna riding Olivia's donkey... Anna being the star of the show...?

It simply hadn't occurred to her when she came back that someone else would be playing Olivia's part. But of course. There had already been new Marys in the years that she'd stayed away. She'd just not seen them, hiding away in her house every year, longing to clap her hands over her ears to blot out the sound of all those Christmas revellers. It had been torture!

It hurt to hear it. It was as if Olivia had been replaced. Had been *forgotten*...

Her chair scraped loudly on the floor as she stood, grabbing her notepad and pen, her bag and coat, and muttering apologies before rushing from the room, feeling sick.

She thought she was on her own. She thought

she would get to her own car in peace. But just as she was inserting her key into the lock of her car she heard her name being called.

'Sydney!'

She didn't want to turn around. She didn't want to be polite and make small talk with whoever it was. She just wanted to go. Surely they wouldn't mind? Surely they'd understand?

She got into her seat and was about to close the door when Nathan appeared at her side, holding the car door so she couldn't close it.

'Hey! Are you okay?'

Why was he here? Why was he even bothering to ask? Why had he come after her?

'I just want to go, Nathan.'

'Something's upset you?'

'No, honestly. I just want to get home, that's all.'

'Is it Lucy? Are you worried about work?'

'No.' She slipped on her seatbelt and stared resolutely out through the windshield rather than looking at him. Her voice softened. 'I'm thrilled for Lucy. Of course I am!'

'Is it me?'

Now she looked at him, her eyes narrowing. 'Why would it be you?'

He shrugged. 'I don't know. Things haven't exactly been…straightforward. There's a…a tension, between us. We didn't exactly get off to the best start, did we?'

'It's not you,' she lied.

'Well, that's good, because they've asked me to work closely with you, seeing as I'm new and you're an established committee member.'

What? When did I miss that bit?

'Oh.'

'That's quite good, really, because—as you heard—Anna came home from school today and told me she's been picked to play the part of Mary. Apparently that means riding a donkey, and she's never done that before, so…'

'So?'

Push the memory away. Don't think about it.

'So we'll need your help.'

He smiled at her. In that way he had. Disarming her and making her feel as if she ought to oblige him with her assistance. His charming eyes twinkling.

'Know any good donkeys? Preferably something that isn't going to buck and break her neck?'

There was someone in the village who kept donkeys. They were used every year for the nativity. And she trusted the animals implicitly.

'Do you know the Bradleys? At Wicklegate Farm?'

He pretended to search his memory. 'Erm...no.'

'Do you know where Wicklegate Farm even *is*?'

He shook his head, smiling. 'No.'

Feeling some of her inner struggle fade, she smiled back. Of course he didn't. 'I suppose I'd better help you, then. Are you free next Saturday?'

'Saturday? All day.'

She nodded and started her engine. 'I'll pick you up at ten in the morning. I know your address. Does Anna have any riding clothes?'

'Er...'

'Anything she doesn't mind getting dirty?'

'My daughter is always happy to wallow in some mud.'

'Good. Tell her I'm going to teach her how to ride a donkey.'

'Thanks.'

He stood back at last, so she could finally close her car door. She was about to drive off, eager to get home, when Nathan rapped his knuckles on her glass.

She pressed the button to wind the window down, letting in the cold evening air. 'What?'

'Lucy's at home. And waiting for your visit.'

She nodded, imagining Lucy in her small cottage, tucked up in bed, looking as proud as Punch with a big smile on her face.

'Has she picked a name for him?'

'I believe she has.'

'What is it?'

He paused, clearly considering whether to say it or not. 'She's named him Oliver.'

Oliver. So close to...

A lump filled her throat and she blinked away tears. Had Lucy chosen that name in honour of her own daughter? If she had, then…

Sydney glanced up at Nathan. 'I'll see you

on Saturday.' And she quickly drove away, before he could see her cry.

Nathan had driven round to Paul and Helen's to check up on them after the accident. They lived on the outskirts of Silverdale and were pretty easy to locate, and he pulled into their driveway feeling optimistic about what he would find. Helen had been released from hospital a while ago and he only needed to remove Paul's stitches from the head laceration.

As he drove in he saw the horse grazing in a field, a blanket wrapped around its body, and smiled. They'd all been very lucky to escape as easily as they had. The accident could have been a lot worse.

But as he pulled up to the house, he spotted another vehicle.

Sydney's.

Why was she here? To check on the horse? It had to be that. It was odd that she was here at the exact same time as him, though.

Just lately she'd been in his thoughts a lot. The universe seemed to be conspiring to throw the two of them together, and whilst he didn't mind that part—she was, after all, a beautiful woman—she did tend to remind him of all his faults and of how he could never be enough for her.

His confidence had taken a knock after Gwyneth's departure. Okay, they'd only been staying in their struggling relationship because she'd learnt she was expecting a baby and Nathan had wanted to be there for her. He'd always had his doubts, and she'd been incredibly high-maintenance, but he'd honestly believed she might change the closer she got to delivering. That they both would.

She hadn't. It had still been, *Me, me, me!*

'Look at all the weight I'm putting on!'

'This pregnancy's giving me acne!'

'I'm getting varicose veins!'

'You do realise after the birth I'm going straight back to work?'

Nathan had reassured her. Had promised her it would be amazing. But it had been *his* dream. Not hers.

It had only been when she'd left him for someone else that he'd realised how much relief he felt. It had stung that she'd left him for someone better. Someone unencumbered by ill health. Someone rich, who could give her the lifestyle she craved. But he'd felt more sorry for his baby girl, who would grow up with a mother who only had enough love for herself.

In the weeks afterwards, when he'd spent hours walking his baby daughter up and down as he tried to get her off to sleep, he'd begun to see how one-sided their relationship had always been.

Gwyneth had always been about appearances. Worrying about whether her hair extensions were the best. Whether her nails needed redoing. How much weight she was carrying. Whether she was getting promoted above someone else. She'd been a social climber—a girl who had been given everything she'd ever wanted by her parents and had come to expect the same in adulthood.

He'd fallen for her glamorous looks and the fact that in the beginning she'd seemed really sweet. But it had all been a snare. A trap. And he'd only begun to see the real Gwyneth when he'd got his diagnosis. Multiple sclerosis had scared her. The idea that she might become nursemaid to a man who wasn't strong, the way she'd pictured him, had *terrified* her.

When Nathan had discovered his illness, and Gwyneth had learned that their perfect life was not so perfect after all, her outlook had changed and she'd said some pretty harsh things. Things he'd taken to heart. That he'd believed.

He didn't want to burden Sydney with any of that.

She'd looked after his daughter for a few hours, she'd looked after and cured their rabbit, she was kind and strong...

She's the sort of woman I would go out with if I could...

But he couldn't.

She'd lost her only daughter. And where was the child's father? From what he'd heard around the village, the father had left them just a couple of months after Olivia had passed away. Shocking them all.

It seemed the whole village had thought the Harpers were strong enough to get through anything. But of course no one could know how such a tragic death would affect them.

Hadn't Sydney been through enough? He had a positive mind-set—even if he did sometimes take the things that Gwyneth had yelled at him to heart. He tried to remain upbeat. But just sometimes his mind would play tricks with him and say, *Yeah, but what if she was right?*

Besides, he wasn't sure he could trust his own judgement about those kinds of things any more. Affairs of the heart. He'd felt so sure about Gwyneth once! In the beginning, anyway. And he'd wanted to do everything for her and the baby. Had wanted the family life that had been right there in front of him. Ready and waiting.

How wrong could he have been?

He'd been floored when she'd left. She'd been high-maintenance, but not once had he suspected that she would react that way to his diagnosis. To having a baby, even. She'd been horrified at what her life had become and had been desperate to escape the drudgery she'd foreseen.

And Nathan had *known* Gwyneth. Or thought he had.

He didn't *know* Sydney. As much as he'd like to.

And he sure as hell didn't want his heart—or Anna's—broken again.

Getting out of the car, he looked up and saw Paul, Helen and Sydney coming out of the house. Helen was standing further back, her arms crossed.

'Dr Jones! Good of you to call round! You've arrived just in time. Your wife was just about to leave.'

He instantly looked at Sydney. My *wife?*

Sydney blushed madly. 'We're not married!'

Paul looked between the two of them. 'Oh, but we thought... Partners, then?'

'No. Just...friends. Associates. We just happened to be in the car together, that's all...' he explained, feeling his voice tail off when he glanced at Sydney's hot face.

'Really? You two look perfect for each other.' Paul smiled.

Nathan was a little embarrassed, but amused at the couple's mistake. 'Hello, Sydney. We seem to keep bumping into each other.'

She shook his hand in greeting. 'We do.'

'Did you get to see Lucy?'

'I did. The baby is gorgeous.'

'He is.' He was still holding her hand. Still looking at her. Someone seemed to have pressed 'pause', because for a moment he lost himself, staring into her grey eyes. It was as if the rest of the world had gone away.

Paul and Helen looked at each other and cleared their throats and Nathan dropped Sydney's hand.

'You're leaving?'

'I just came to check on the horse. No after-effects from the accident.'

'That's good. How about you, Paul? Any head-aches? Anything I should be worried about?'

'No, Doc. All well and good, considering.'

'How about you, Helen?'

'I'm fine. Physically.'

'That's good.'

Sydney pulled her car keys from her pocket. 'Well, I must dash. Good to see you all so well. Paul. Helen.' She looked over at Nathan, her gaze lingering longer than it should. 'Dr Jones.'

He watched her go. Watched as she started her engine, reversed, turned and drove out of the driveway. He even watched as her car disappeared out of sight, up the lane.

Suddenly remembering that he was there to see Paul and Helen, he turned back to them, feeling embarrassed. 'Shall we go in? Get those stitches seen to?'

Paul nodded, draping his arm around Nathan's shoulder conspiratorially. 'Just friends, huh?'

He felt his cheeks colour. They'd caught him watching her. Seen how distracted she made him.

'Just friends.'

Inside the house, Helen disappeared into the kitchen to make a cup of tea.

'So, Paul… How are you?' He noted the stitches in his scalp. He'd certainly got a nasty laceration there, but apart from that obvious injury he seemed quite well.

'I'm good, Doc, thanks.' Paul settled into the chair opposite.

They had a lovely home. It was a real country cottage, with lots of character and tons of original features. There was a nice fire crackling away in the fireplace. It looked as if they were in the process of putting some Christmas decorations up.

'So I need to remove your stitches. How many days have they been in?'

'Too long! I'm really grateful for you coming out like this. I was going to make an appointment to come and say thanks to you. For saving me and Helen. And Brandon, too, of course.'

'It wasn't a problem. We were just in the right place at the right time.'

'You were in the perfect place.' He looked down at the floor and then got his next words out in a quiet rush, after he'd turned to check that Helen wasn't listening. 'Helen and I didn't see that deer coming across the field because we were arguing.'

'Oh?' Nathan sensed a confession coming.

'I…er…hadn't reacted very well to the fact that…well…' He looked uncomfortable. 'Helen had had a miscarriage. Two weeks earlier. The hospital said they'd send you a letter… We hadn't even known she was pregnant, but she had this bleed that wouldn't stop, and we ended up at A&E one night, and they found out it was an incomplete miscarriage. She needed a D&C.'

Nathan felt a lurch in his stomach. 'I'm very sorry to hear that.'

'Yeah, well…apparently *I* wasn't sorry enough. Helen got mad with me because I wasn't upset about losing the baby. But neither of us had even *known* about the pregnancy! How could I get upset over a baby I didn't know about?' Paul let out a heavy breath. 'She thought I didn't care. We were arguing about that. Yelling…screaming at each other—so much so that Brandon started too. We didn't notice the deer because I wasn't paying attention.' He sounded guilty. 'And now, because I didn't notice the deer running in front of us, and because I didn't notice my wife was pregnant, *I'm* the bad guy who nearly got us all killed.'

How awful for them! To lose a baby like that and then to have a serious accident on top of it. They were both very lucky to have got out alive. Brandon, too. It could all have gone so terribly wrong.

'Well, I can sort your stitches for you. And I'm not so sure I would *want* to stop Helen being mad. She's had a terrible loss, Paul. You both have. And she needs to work through it.'

'I know, but…'

'There are support groups. Ones specifically for women who have suffered miscarriage. I can give you some information if you drop by the surgery. Or maybe I could ask Helen if she wants to come in and have a chat with me? You may not have known about the pregnancy, but she still lost a baby. A D&C can be a traumatic event in itself, when you think about what it is, and it can help some women to talk about things. She's had a loss and she needs to work her way through it. And I'm sure, in time, so will you.'

Paul rubbed at his bristly jaw. 'But even *she* didn't know.'

'It doesn't matter. It was still a baby, Paul. Still a loss. A terrible one. And she knows *now*. She probably feels a lot of guilt, and the easiest person to take that out on is you.'

'Does she think *I've* not been hurt too? To not even know she was pregnant and then to see her so scared when she wouldn't stop bleeding? And then to learn the reason why?' He shook his head, tears welling in his eyes. '*Why* didn't I know?'

'You're not to blame. It's difficult in those early weeks.'

'I keep thinking there must have something else I could have done for her. Something I could have said. To see that pain in her eyes… It broke my heart.'

Nathan laid a hand on Paul's shoulder.

'It *has* hurt me. I *am* upset. And I feel guilty at trying to make her get over something when she's just not ready to. Guilty that I won't get to hold that baby in my arms…'

'Grief takes time to heal. For both of you.'

Paul glanced at his hands. 'But she won't talk to me. She doesn't talk to me about any of the deep stuff because she thinks I don't care. She never shares what she's feeling. How are you supposed to be in a relationship with someone who won't tell you what's really going on?'

With great difficulty.

He looked at Paul. 'You wait. Until she's ready. And when she is…you listen.'

Nathan was so glad he'd never had to go through

something like this with Gwyneth. They'd come close, when she'd thought there might still be time for an abortion, but the thought of losing his child…? It was too terrible even to think about.

Sydney would understand.

Just thinking about her now made him realise just how strong she was to have got through her daughter's death. And on her own, too.

'So I've just got to take her anger, then?'

'Be there for her. Be ready to talk when she is. She's grieving.'

Was Sydney still grieving? Was that why she wasn't able to talk to him about what had happened? Should he even *expect* her to open up to him?

He opened his doctor's bag and pulled out a small kit to remove Paul's stitches. There were ten of them, and he used a stitch-cutter and tweezers to hold the knots each time he removed them. The wound had healed well, but Paul would be left with a significant scar for a while.

'That's you done.'

'Thanks. So I've just got to wait it out, then?'

'Or you could raise the subject if *you* feel the

need. I can see that you're upset at the loss, too. Let her know she can talk to you. That you're ready to talk whenever she is.'

Paul nodded and touched the spot where his stitches had been. 'Maybe I will. I know I've lost a baby, but I'm even more scared of losing my wife.'

Nathan just stared back at him.

Sydney felt odd. She had to call round to Nathan's house in a minute, so she could take them to Wicklegate Farm and teach Anna how to ride the donkey. But for some reason she was standing in front of her wardrobe, wondering what to wear?

It shouldn't matter!

Deliberately she grabbed at a pair of old jeans, an old rugby shirt that was slightly too big for her and thick woolly socks to wear inside her boots.

I have no reason to dress up for Dr Jones.

However, once dressed, she found herself staring at her reflection in the mirror, messing with her hair. Up? Down?

She decided to leave her hair down and then

added a touch of make-up. A bit of blush. Some mascara.

Her reflection stared back at her in question.

What are you doing?

Her mirror image gave no response. Obviously. But that still didn't stop her waiting for one, hoping she would see something in the mirror that would tell her the right thing to do.

She even looked at Magic. 'Am I being stupid about this?'

Magic blinked slowly at her.

She *liked* Nathan, and that was the problem. She liked it that he was comfortable to be with. She liked it that he was great to talk to. That he was very easy on the eye.

There was some small security in the fact that his little girl would be there, so it was hardly going to be a seduction, but... But a part of her—a small part, admittedly—wondered what it would be like if something were to happen with them spending time together. What, though? A kiss? On the cheek? *The lips?* That small part of her wanted to know what it would feel like to close her eyes and feel his lips press against hers.

To inhale his scent, to feel his hands upon her. To sink into his strong caress.

Alastair, in those last few months, made me feel like I had the plague. That I was disgusting to him. It would be nice to know that a man could still find me desirable.

She missed that physical connection with someone. She missed having someone in her bed in the morning. Someone to read the papers with. To talk to over a meal. She missed the comfort of sitting in the same room as another person and not even having to talk. Of sharing a good book recommendation, of watching a movie together snuggled under an old quilt and feeding each other popcorn. Coming home and not finding the house empty.

But so what? Just because she missed it, it didn't mean she had to make it happen. No matter how much she fantasised about it. Nathan was a man. And in her experience men let you down. Especially when you needed them the most. She'd already been rejected once, when she was at her lowest, and she didn't want to go through that again.

It was too hard.

So no matter how nice Nathan was—no matter how attractive, no matter how much she missed being *held*—nothing was going to happen. Today was about Anna. About donkeys and learning how to ride.

She remembered teaching Olivia. It had taken her ages to get her balance, and she'd needed a few goes at it before she'd felt confident. She hadn't liked pulling at the reins, had been worried in case it hurt the donkey.

Thinking about the past made her think of the present. Her ex-husband, Alastair, had moved on. He'd found someone new. Was making a new family. How had he moved on so quickly? It was almost insulting. Had she meant nothing to him? Had the family they'd had meant less to him than she'd realised? Perhaps that was why he'd walked away so easily?

Everyone in the village had been shocked. *Everyone*. Well, she'd make sure that everyone knew *she* wasn't moving on. Keeping Nathan and Anna at arm's length was the right thing to do, despite what she was feeling inside.

She considered cancelling. Calling him and apologising. Telling him that an emergency had cropped up. But then she'd realised that if she did she would still have to meet him again at some point. It was best to get it over and done with straight away. Less dilly-dallying. Besides, she didn't want to let Anna down. She was a good kid.

She held her house keys in her hand for a moment longer, debating with her inner conscience, and her gaze naturally strayed to a photograph of Olivia. She was standing with her head back, looking up to the sun, her eyes closed, smiling at the feel of warmth on her face. It was one of Sydney's favourite pictures: Olivia embracing the warmth of the sun.

She always enjoyed life. Even the small things.

Sydney stepped outside and locked up the cottage. She needed to drive to Nathan's house. The new estate and the road he lived on was about two miles away.

It was interesting to drive through the new builds. The houses were very modern, in bright brick, with cool grey slate tiles on their roofs and shiny white UPVC windows. They were uniformly identical, but she could see Nathan's muddy jalopy parked on his driveway and she pulled in behind it, letting out a breath. Releasing her nerves.

I can do this!

She strode up to the front door, trying to look businesslike, hoping that no one could see how nervous she suddenly felt inside. She rang the bell and let out a huge breath, trying to calm her scattered nerves.

The door opened and Nathan stood there. Smiling. 'Sydney—hi. Come on in.' he stepped back.

Reluctant to enter his home, and therefore create feelings of intimacy, she stepped back. 'Erm...shouldn't we just be off? I told the owners we'd be there in about ten minutes.'

'I'm just waiting for Anna to finish getting ready. You know what young girls are like.'

She watched his cheeks colour as he realised what he'd said, and to let him off the hook decided to step in, but keeping herself as far away from him physically as she could.

'I do...yes. Anna?' she called up the stairs.

Sydney heard some thumps and bumps and then Anna was at the top of the stairs. 'Hi, Sydney! I can't decide what to wear. Could you help me? *Please?*'

Anna wheedled out the last word, giving the cutest face that she could.

The look was so reminiscent of Olivia that Sydney had to catch her breath.

'Erm…' she glanced at Nathan, who shrugged.

'By all means…'

'Right.'

Sydney ascended the stairs, feeling sweat break out down her spine. She turned at the top and went into Anna's room. Her breath was taken away by how *girly* it was. A palace of pink. A pink feather boa hung over the mirror on a dresser, there were fairy lights around the headboard, bubblegum-coloured beanbags, a blushpink carpet and curtains, a hammock in the corner filled with all manner of soft, cuddly toys and a patchwork quilt upon the bed.

And in front of a large pink wardrobe that had a crenelated top, like a castle, Anna stood, one hand on one hip, the other tapping her finger against her lips.

'I've never ridden a donkey. Or a horse! I don't know what would be best.'

Sydney swallowed hard as she eyed the plethora of clothes in every colour under the sun. 'Erm… something you don't mind getting dirty. Trousers or jeans. And a tee shirt? Maybe a jumper?'

Anna pulled out a mulberry-coloured jumper that was quite a thick knit, with cabling down the front. 'Like this?'

Syd nodded. 'Perfect. Trousers?'

'I have these.' Anna pulled a pair of jeans from a pile. They had some diamanté sequins sewn around the pockets. 'And this?' She pointed at the tee shirt she was already wearing.

'Those will be great. I'll go downstairs whilst you're getting dressed.'

'Could you help me, Sydney? I can never do the buttons.'

Sydney stood awkwardly whilst Anna changed her clothes, and then knelt in front of the little girl to help her do up her clothes. It had been ages since she'd had to do this. Olivia had always struggled with buttons. These two girls might almost have been made out of the same mould. Of course there were so differences between the girls, but sometimes the similarities were disturbing. Painful.

She stood up again. 'Ready?'

Anna nodded and dashed by her to run downstairs. 'I'll get my boots on!'

She sat at the bottom of the stairs and pulled on bright green wellington boots that had comical frog eyes poking out over the toes.

Sydney stood behind her, looking awkwardly at Nathan.

'Will I need boots, too?' he asked.

She nodded. 'It's a working farm…so, yes.'

She watched as they both got ready, and it was so reminiscent of standing waiting for Olivia and Alastair to get ready so they could go out that she physically felt an ache in her chest.

They had been good together. Once. When she and Alastair had married she'd truly believed they would be in each other's arms until their last days. Shuffling along together. One of those old couples you could see in parks, still holding hands.

But then it had all gone wrong.

Alastair hadn't been able to cope with losing his little girl and he'd blamed her. For not noticing that Olivia was truly ill. For not acting sooner. The way he'd blanked her, directed his anger towards her, had hurt incredibly. The one time she'd needed her husband the most had been the one time he'd failed her completely.

When Nathan and Anna were both ready she hurried them out of the door and got them into her car.

'Can you do your seatbelt, Anna?'

'Yes!' the little girl answered, beaming. 'I can't wait to ride the donkey! Did Daddy tell you I'm going to be Mary? That's the most important part in the play. Well…except for baby Jesus…but that's just going to be a doll, so…' She trailed off.

Sydney smiled into the rearview mirror. How many times had she driven her car with Olivia babbling away in the back seat? Too many times. So often, in fact, that she would usually be thinking about all the things she had to do, tuning her daughter out, saying *hmm*...or *right*...in all the right places, whenever her daughter paused for breath.

And now...? With Anna chatting away...? She wanted to listen. Wanted to show Nathan's little girl that she heard her.

I can't believe I ignored my daughter! Even for a second!

How many times had she not truly listened? How many times had she not paid attention? Thinking that she had all the time in the world to talk to her whenever she wanted? To chat about things that hadn't meant much to her but had meant the world to her daughter?

'All eyes will be on you, Anna. I'm sure you'll do a great job.'

Nathan glanced over at her. 'I appreciate you arranging this. I don't suppose you're a dab hand with a sewing machine, are you?'

She was, actually. 'Why?'

'The costume for Mary is looking a bit old. The last incumbent seems to have dragged it through a dump before storing it away and now it looks awful. Miriam has suggested that I make another one.'

She glanced over at him. 'And you said…?'

'I said yes! But that was when I thought a bedsheet and a blue teacloth over the head was all that was needed.'

'You know… I might still have Olivia's old outfit. She played Mary one year.'

'She did?' Nathan was looking at her closely.

'I still have some of her stuff in boxes in the attic. Couldn't bear to part with it. Give me a day or two and I'll check.'

'That's very kind of you.'

She kept her eyes on the road, trying not to think too hard about going up into the attic to open those boxes. Would the clothes still have Olivia's scent? Would seeing them, touching them, be too painful? There was a reason they were still in the attic. Unsorted.

She'd boxed everything up one day, after a therapist at one of her grief counselling sessions had told her it might be a good thing to do. That it might be cathartic, or something.

It hadn't been.

She'd felt that in boxing up her daughter's clothes and putting them somewhere they couldn't be seen she was also been getting rid of all traces of her daughter. That she was hiding Olivia's memory away. And she'd not been ready. She'd drunk an awful lot of wine that night, and had staggered up into the attic to drag all the boxes back downstairs, but Alastair had stopped her. Yelled at her that it was a *good* thing, and that if she touched those boxes one more time then he would walk out the door.

She'd sobered up and the next morning had left the boxes up there—even though she'd felt bereft and distraught. And dreadfully hungover.

Alastair had left eventually, of course. Just not then. It had taken a few more weeks. By then it had been too late to drag the boxes back down. Too scary.

'What was she like?'

'Hmm?' She was pulled back to the present by his question. 'What?'

'What was Olivia like?' he asked again.

She glanced over at him quickly. He sounded as if he really wanted to know, and no one had asked her that question for years. All this time she'd stayed away from people, not making connections or getting close because she hadn't wanted to talk about Olivia. It had been too painful. But now she *wanted* to talk about her. Was thrilled that he'd asked, because she was *ready* to talk about her. He'd made it easy to do so.

'She was…amazing.'

'Who's Olivia?' asked Anna from the back seat.

Sydney glanced in the rearview mirror once again and smiled.

The donkey was called Bert and he had a beautiful dark brown coat. The farmer had already got him saddled before their arrival and he stood waiting patiently, nibbling at some hay, as Sydney gave Anna instructions.

'Okay, it's quite simple, Anna. You don't need Bert to go fast, so you don't need to nudge him with your feet or kick at his sides. A slow plod is what we want, and Bert here is an expert at the slow plod and the Christmas nativity.'

'Will he bite me?'

She shook her head. 'No. He's very gentle and

he is used to children riding him. Shall I lift you into the saddle?'

Anna nodded.

Sydney hefted Anna up. 'Put your hands here, on the pommel. I'll lead him with the reins—the way we'll get the boy playing Joseph to do it.'

'Okay.'

'Verbal commands work best, and Bert responds to *Go on* when you want him to start walking and *Stop* when you want him to stand still. Got that?'

Anna nodded again.

'Why don't you give that a try?'

Anna smiled. 'Go on, Bert!'

Bert started moving.

'He's doing it, Sydney! He's *doing* it! Look, Daddy—I'm riding!'

'That's brilliant, sweetheart.'

Sydney led Bert down the short side of the field. She turned to check on Anna. 'That's it. Keep your back straight...don't slouch.'

They walked up and down. Up and down. Until Sydney thought Anna was ready to try and do it on her own. She'd certainly picked it up a lot more quickly than Olivia had!

'Okay, Anna. Try it on your own. Head to the end of the field and use the reins to turn him and make him come back. Talk to him. Encourage him. Okay?'

She knew Anna could do it. The little girl had connected with the donkey in a way no other had, and the animal responded brilliantly to her. Sydney really didn't think Anna would have a problem on the night of the nativity. Bert was putty in her hands.

They both stood and watched as Anna led Bert confidently away from them and down the field. Sydney almost felt proud. In fact, she *was* proud.

She became aware that Nathan was staring at her, and then suddenly, almost in a blink, she felt his fingers sliding around hers.

'Thank you, Sydney.'

She turned to him and looked into his eyes. The intensity of the moment grew. It felt as if her heart had sped up but her breathing had got really slow. Her fingers in his felt protected and safe, and he stroked the back of her hand with his thumb in slow, sweeping strokes that were doing strange, chaotic things to her insides, turning her legs to jelly.

'What for?' she managed to say.

'For helping me when it's difficult for you. I appreciate the time you're giving me and my daughter. I...'

He stopped talking as he took a step closer to her, and as he drew near her breathing stopped completely and she looked up into his handsome blue eyes.

He's going to kiss me!

Hadn't she thought about this? Hadn't she wondered what it might be like? Hadn't she missed the physical contact that came with being in a relationship? And now here was this man—this incredibly *attractive* man—holding her hand and making her stomach do twirls and swirls as his lips neared hers, as he leaned in for a kiss...

Sydney closed her eyes, awaiting the press of his lips against hers.

Only there was no kiss.

She felt him pull his hand free from hers and heard him clearing his throat and apologising before he called out, 'You're doing brilliantly, Anna! Turn him round now—come on. We need to go home.'

Sydney blinked. What had happened? He'd been about to kiss her, hadn't he? And she'd stood there, like an idiot, waiting for him to do it.

How embarrassing!

Anna brought Bert to a halt beside them, beaming widely.

'I think that's enough for today. You've done really well, Anna.'

Anna beamed as her father helped her off the donkey, and then she ran straight to Sydney and wrapped her arms around her. 'Thanks, Sydney! You're the best!'

Sydney froze at the unexpected hug, but then she relaxed and hugged the little girl back, swallowing back her surprise and…for some reason… her tears. 'So are you.'

The farmer took Bert back to his field with the other donkeys, once he'd removed the saddle and tack, and Sydney and Anna said goodbye. Then they all got back into Sydney's car and she started to drive them home.

'Thank you for…er…what you've done for Anna today,' said Nathan.

She took a breath and bit back the retort she wanted to give. 'No problem.'

'You know…taking time out of your weekend…'

'Sydney could stay for dinner, couldn't she Daddy? We're having fajitas!' Anna invited from the back.

She would have loved nothing more than to stay. Her time spent with Anna had been wonderful, and the times when she'd looked across at Nathan and caught him looking at her had been weirdly wonderful and exciting too.

But after what had just happened—the almost-kiss… He'd been going to do it. She knew it! But something had stopped him. Had got in the way.

Was it because he'd suddenly remembered Anna was there? Had he not wanted to risk his daughter seeing them kissing? Or was it something else?

She was afraid of getting carried away and reading too much into this situation. She'd helped out. That was all. She'd felt a connection that Nathan hadn't. Getting too involved with this single dad was perhaps a step too far. Where would it end? If she spent too much time with them, where would she be?

She shivered, even though the car heater was pumping out plenty of hot air. 'I'm sorry, I can't. I've got a…a thing later.'

'Maybe another time?' Nathan suggested, looking embarrassed.

As well you might!

'Sure.'

There can't ever be another time, no.

She watched them clamber from her car when she dropped them off. Nathan lingered at the open window of the car, as if he had something else to say, but then he looked away and simply said goodbye, before following his daughter up the path.

Sydney drove off before he could turn around and say anything else.

I really like them. Both of them.

But was it what they represented that she liked? This dad. This little girl. They were a ready-made family. Being with them might give her back some of what she'd lost. They offered a chance of starting again. So was it the *situation* that she liked? Or *them* as individuals?

Nathan was great. Gorgeous, charming, someone she enjoyed being around. And Anna was cute as a button, with her sing-song voice and happy-go-lucky personality.

Was it wrong to envy them? To envy them because they still had each other?

Was it wrong to have wanted—to have *craved*—Nathan's kiss?

Feeling guilty, she drove home, and she was just about to park up when she got a text. A cat was having difficulties giving birth and she needed to get to the surgery immediately to prep for a Caesarean section.

Suddenly all business—which was easy because she knew what she was doing—she turned the car around and drove to the surgery.

Nathan sent Anna upstairs to get changed into some clean clothes that didn't smell of donkey and farm. Then he headed into the kitchen, switching on the kettle and sinking into a chair as he waited for it to boil.

What the hell had he done?

Something crazy—something not *him*—had somehow slipped through his defences and he'd found himself taking hold of Sydney's hand, staring into her sad grey eyes. And he had been about to *kiss her*!

Okay, so he'd been fighting that urge for a while, and it was hardly a strange impulse, but he *had* thought that he'd got those impulses under control.

Standing there, looking down into her face, at her smooth skin, her slightly rosy cheeks, those soft, inviting lips, he'd wanted to so badly! And she'd wanted him to do it. He'd wanted to, but...

But Anna hadn't been far away, and he'd suddenly heard that horrid voice in his head that still sounded remarkably like Gwyneth, telling him that no one, and especially not Sydney, would want him. Not with his faulty, failing body. Not with his bad genes. Not with a child who wasn't hers...

How could he ask her to take on that burden—

especially with the threat of his MS always present? He knew the chances of the MS killing him were practically zero. Okay, there would be difficulties, and there would be complications—there might even be comorbidities such as thyroid disease, autoimmune conditions or a meningioma. But the MS on its own...? It was unlikely.

But it had been enough to make him hesitate. To think twice. And once he'd paused too long he'd known it was too late to kiss her so he'd stepped away. Had called out to Anna...said they needed to go.

Sydney deserved a strong man. A man who would look out for her and care for her and protect her. What if he couldn't do that?

Fear. That was what it had been. Fear of putting himself out there. Of getting involved. Of exposing himself to the hurt and pain that Gwyneth had caused once. How could he go through again? How could he expose Anna to that now that she was older? She would be aware now if she grew to love someone and then that someone decided it was all too much and wanted out.

Anna being a baby had protected her from

the pain of losing her mother. And today he had saved himself from finding out if he could be enough for someone like Sydney. Gwyneth had made him doubt what he had to offer. She had probably been right in what she'd said. He didn't know what his future would be like. He couldn't be certain, despite trying his best to remain positive. But it was hard sometimes. Dealing with a chronic illness…sometimes it could get to you.

The kettle boiled and he slowly made himself a cup of tea. He heard Anna come trotting back down the stairs and she came into the kitchen.

'Can I have a biscuit, Daddy?'

'Just one.'

She reached into the biscuit barrel and took out a plain biscuit. 'I loved riding Bert. He was so cute! I love donkeys. Do *you* love donkeys, Daddy?'

He thought for a moment. 'I do. Especially Bert.'

She smiled at him, crumbs dropping onto the floor. 'And do you love Sydney?'

His gaze swung straight round to his daughter's face. 'What?'

'I think you like her.'

'What makes you say that?' he asked in a stran-gled voice.

'Your eyes go all funny.' She giggled. 'Joshua in my class—he looks at Gemma like that and he *loves* her. They're boyfriend and girlfriend.'

Nathan cleared his throat. 'Aren't they a little young to be boyfriend and girlfriend?'

Anna shrugged, and then skipped off into the other room. He heard the television go on.

She noticed quite a lot, did Anna.

Curious, he followed her through to the lounge and stood and watched her for a moment as she chose a channel to watch.

'Anna?'

'Yes?'

'If I did like Sydney…how would you feel about that?'

Anna tilted her head to one side and smiled, before turning back to the television. 'Fine. Then you wouldn't be all alone.'

Nathan stared at his daughter. And smiled.

CHAPTER SIX

IT HAD BEEN a long time since Sydney had had to play 'mother', and now she had the pleasure once again. The cat she'd raced to had recovered from its surgery, but had disowned her kittens afterwards. It happened sometimes with animals, when they missed giving birth in the traditional way and there just wasn't that bond there for them.

The four kittens—three black females and a black and white male—were kicking off their December in a small cat carrier at her home and she was on round-the-clock feeding every two hours.

Sydney was quite enjoying it. It gave her purpose. It gave her a routine. But mostly it gave her something to do during the long hours of the lonely nights. Even if she *was* still torturing herself with what might have happened between her and Nathan.

I wanted him to kiss me and I made that perfectly clear!

She'd hardly fought it, had she? Standing there all still, eyes closed, awaiting his kiss like some stupid girl in a fairytale. He must have thought she was a right sap. Perhaps that was what had put him off...

Disturbed from her reverie by the sound of her doorbell, she glanced at the clock—it was nearly eight in the morning—and went to answer the door.

It didn't cross her mind that she'd been up all night, hadn't combed her hair or washed her face, or that she was still wearing yesterday's clothes and smelt slightly of antiseptic and donkey at the same time.

She opened the door to see Nathan and Anna standing there. 'Er... Hi... Sorry, had we arranged to meet?' She felt confused by their being there. And so early, too.

'We were out getting breakfast,' Nathan explained. 'Anna wanted croissants and jam. We didn't have any and...' He blinked, squirming slightly. 'I thought you might like to share some with us.'

He raised a brown paper bag that was starting to show grease spots and she suddenly realised how hungry she was.

Her mouth watered and her stomach ached for the food and nourishment. Warm, buttery croissants sounded delicious!

Even though she still felt embarrassed after yesterday, the lure of the food overpowered the feeling.

'Sure. Come on in.' She stepped back, biting her lip as they passed, wondering if she was making a huge mistake in accepting. Hadn't this man humiliated her just yesterday? Unintentionally, perhaps, but still... And today she was letting him in to her house? She had no idea where her boundaries were with them any more.

Following the scent of food to her kitchen, she washed her hands and got out some plates, then butter from the fridge.

'I don't have any jam...'

'We do!' Anna chirruped. 'Blackberry, apricot

and strawberry!' She put a small bag holding the jars onto the kitchen counter.

Sydney nodded. 'Wow! You *do* come prepared, don't you? There can't be many people wandering around with a full condiments selection.'

Nathan grinned. 'We weren't sure which one you liked, so...'

He was trying to say sorry. She could see that. The croissants, the jam, the sudden breakfast—these were all part of his white flag. His olive branch. His truce. She would be cruel to reject it. Especially as it was going to be so nice. When had she last had a breakfast like this?

'I like apricot, so thank you for getting it for me.'

She smiled and mussed Anna's hair, and then indicated they should all sit at the table. Sydney filled the kettle, and poured some juice for Anna, and then they all settled down to eat.

Her home was filled with laughter, flaky pastries and the wonderful sound of happiness. It was as if her kitchen had been waiting for this family to fill it, and suddenly it no longer seemed the cold empty room she knew, but a room full of life and purpose and identity.

For an hour she forgot her grief. She let down her barriers and her walls and allowed them in. Despite her uncertainty, they were good for her. Anna was wonderfully bright and cheerful and giggly. And those differences between her and Olivia were growing starker by the minute. Anna liked looking at flowers, but had no interest in growing them. She knew what she wanted to be when she was grown up. She liked building things and being hands-on. She was such a sweet little girl, and so endearing, and Nathan...

They just got on well together. It was easy for them all.

Sydney was licking the last of the croissant crumbs from her fingers when Nathan said, 'How come you don't have any Christmas decorations?'

His question was like a bucket of ice-cold water being thrown over her. It was a reality check. It pulled her back to her *actual* life and not the temporarily happy one she'd been enjoying.

'I don't do Christmas.'

He held her gaze, trying to see beyond her words. Trying to learn her reasons.

Anna looked at her in shock. 'Don't you believe in Santa Claus?'

Sydney smiled at her. If only it were that simple. 'Of course I do. Santa is a very good reason to enjoy Christmas.' She thought for a moment. 'Anna, why don't you go and take a look at what's in the blue cat carrier in my lounge? Be gentle, though.'

Anna gasped and ran into the other room, and Sydney turned back to face Nathan. She sucked in a breath to speak but nothing came out. Thankfully he didn't judge or say anything. He just waited for her to speak. And suddenly she could.

'Olivia died just before Christmas. It seems wrong to celebrate it.'

He swallowed. 'Do you want to talk about it?'

She did...but after the way he'd been with her yesterday... Did she want to share the innermost pain in her heart with a man who could blow so hot and cold? What would be the point in telling him if he wasn't going to stick around? If he wasn't going to be the kind of person she needed in her life? Because she was beginning to think that maybe there *could* be someone. One day. Maybe.

Could the person be Nathan?

She didn't want to feel vulnerable again, or helpless. But sitting in her home night after night, *alone*, was making her feel more vulnerable than she'd ever realised. Yet still she wasn't sure whether to tell him everything.

He stared at her intently, focusing on her eyes, her lips, then on her eyes again. What was he trying to see? What was he trying to decide?

He soon let her know, by confiding something of his own.

'I have MS—multiple sclerosis. To be exact, I have relapsing remitting multiple sclerosis. I have attacks of symptoms that come on suddenly and then go away again.'

She leaned forward, concerned. Intrigued. Was this what had been wrong with him the other day? When he'd been all dizzy at the veterinary surgery? And that time at the accident site?

'MS...?'

'I was diagnosed the week before Anna was

born. It was a huge shock—nothing compared to losing a child, but it had tremendous repercussions. Not only my life, but Anna's too. Anna's mother walked out on us both during a time in which I was already reeling. Only a couple of weeks after we'd had Anna, Gwyneth left us… but it doesn't stop us from celebrating Anna's birthday each year. She gets presents, a cake, a party, balloons. You *should* enjoy Christmas. You *should* celebrate. There aren't many times in our lives where we can really enjoy ourselves, but Christmas is one of them.'

Sydney stood up and began to clear away the breakfast things. She'd heard what he'd said, but his story hardly touched hers. 'That's completely different.'

He got up and followed her into the kitchen, grabbed her arm. 'No, it isn't.'

She yanked her arm free. 'Yes, it is! My child *died*. Your girlfriend walked out. There's a *big* difference.'

'Sydney—'

'Do you think I can *enjoy* being reminded every year that my daughter is dead? Every time

Christmas begins—and it seems to get earlier every year—everywhere I look people are putting up decorations and trees and lights, buying presents for each other, and they're all in a happy mood. All I can see is my daughter, lying in a hospital bed with tubes coming out of her, and myself being told that I need to say goodbye! Do you have *any* idea of how that feels? To know that everybody else is *happy* because it's that time of year again?'

He shook his head. 'No. I couldn't possibly know.'

'No.' She bit back her tears and slumped against the kitchen units, lost in memories of that hospital once again. Feeling the old, familiar pain and grief. 'I became the saddest I could ever be at this time of year—when everyone else is at their happiest. I can't sleep. It's hard for me. I could *never* celebrate.'

Nathan stood in front of her and took one of her hands in his, looking down at their interlocked fingers. 'Perhaps you need to stop focusing on the day that she died and instead start focusing on all the days that she lived...'

His words stunned her. A swell of anger like a giant wave washed over her and she had to reach out to steady herself. It was that powerful.

How *dared* he tell her how she ought to grieve? How she ought to remember her daughter! He had no idea of how she felt and here he was—another *doctor*—telling her what she needed to do, handing out advice.

She inhaled a deep breath through her nose, feeling her shoulders rise up and her chin jut out in defiance as she stared at him, feeling her fury seethe out from her every pore.

'Get out.'

'Sydney—'

He tried to reach for her arm, but seeing his hand stretched out towards her, without her permission, made her feel even more fury and she batted him away.

'You don't get to tell me how to deal with my grief. You don't get to tell me how I should be thinking. You don't get to tell me anything!'

She stormed away from him—out of her kitchen, down the hallway, towards her front door, which she wrenched open. Then she stood there, arms folded, as tears began to break and her bottom lip began to wobble with the force of her anger and upset.

She felt as if she could tackle anything with the strength of feeling she had inside her right now. Wrestle a lion? *Bring it on.* Take down a giant? *Bring it on.* Chuck someone out of her home? *Bring. It. On!*

Nathan followed her, apology written all over his features. 'Look, Syd, I'm sorry. I—'

She held up a finger, ignoring the fact that it was shaking and trembling with her rage. 'Don't. Don't you *dare.* I don't want to hear any of it. Not from you. You with your *"drink warm milk"* advice and your *"why not try grief counselling?"* and your *"focus on the days she lived"* advice. You couldn't *possibly* understand what I am going through! You couldn't even kiss me, Dr Nathan Jones, so you don't get to tell me how to live.'

He stared back at her, his Adam's apple bobbing up and down as he swallowed hard. Then he sighed and called out for his daughter. 'Anna? We need to go.'

They both heard Anna make a protest at having to leave. She was obviously having far too much fun with the orphaned kittens.

But she showed up in the doorway and looked at both her father and Sydney. 'Are we leaving?'

''Fraid so.' Nathan nodded and gave her a rueful smile. 'We need to head back now. Sydney's got things to do.'

'Not fair, Daddy! I want to stay with the kittens. Sydney, can I stay for a little bit—*pleeeeeease*?' She added a sickly sweet smile and clutched her hands before her like she was begging for a chance of life before a judge.

Nathan steered her out through the front door. 'Another time, honey.' As he moved out of the door he turned briefly to Sydney. 'I'm sorry I've upset you. I didn't mean anything by it.'

She closed the door, and as it slammed, as she shut out the sight of Nathan and Anna walking away down her front path, she sank to the floor and put her head in her hands and sobbed. Huge, gulping sobs. Sobs that caused her to hiccup. Sobs that took ages to fade away, leaving her crouched in the hallway just breathing in a silence broken only by the ticking clock.

Finally she was able to get to her feet, and listlessly she headed back to the kitchen to clear away the breakfast things.

Sydney had felt numb for a few hours. It was a strange feeling. Having got that angry, that upset, it was as if she'd used up a year's worth of emotions all in a few minutes, and now her body and her mind had become completely exhausted, unable to feel anything.

Now she sat in her empty home, looking at the pictures of her daughter, and felt...*nothing*. No sadness. No joy. She couldn't even bring herself to try and remember the days on which they'd been taken, and when she tried to remember the sound of her daughter's chuckles she couldn't conjure it up.

It was like being frozen. Or as if she could move, breathe, live, exist, but the rest of the world was seen through a filter somehow. It was as if her memories were gone—as if her feelings had been taken away and in their place a giant nothingness remained.

She didn't like it. It made her feel even more isolated than she had been before. Lonely. She didn't even have her daughter's memories to accompany her in the silence.

She wasn't ready to forget her daughter. To lose her. She needed to remind herself again. To reconnect.

Sydney looked up. Olivia's things were in the attic. Her clothes. Her toys. Her books. Everything. She hadn't been able to go up in the loft for years because of them, but perhaps she needed to at this moment.

So, despite the tiredness and the lethargy taking over every limb, muscle and bone, she headed up the stairs and opened up the attic, sliding down the metal ladder and taking a deep breath before she headed up the steps.

There was a stillness in the attic. As if she'd entered a sacred, holy space. But instead of vaulted ceilings with regal columns and priceless holy relics gleaming in soft sunlight there was loft insulation, piles of boxes and a single bulb that was lit by pulling a hanging chain.

She let out a long, slow breath as some of her numbness began to dissipate, and in its place she felt a nervous anxiety begin to build.

Was she right to be doing this? She hadn't looked through these things for so long!

Am I strong enough? What if it's too much?

But then there was another voice in her head. A logical voice.

It's only clothes. Books. Toys. Nothing here can hurt you.

Doubt told her that something might. But she edged towards the first box, labelled *'Costumes'*, and began to unfold the top, not realising that she was biting into her bottom lip until she felt a small pain.

The contents of the box were topped with taffeta. A dress of some sort. Sydney lifted it out to look at it, to try and force a memory. And this time it came.

Olivia had wanted a 'princess dress' for a party. They'd gone shopping into Norton town centre together, her daughter holding on to her hand as she'd skipped alongside her. They'd gone from shop to shop, looking for the perfect dress, and she'd spotted this one. With a beautiful purple velvet bodice and reams upon reams of lilac taffeta billowing out from the waist.

Olivia had looked perfect in it! Twirling in front of the mirror, this way and that, swishing the skirt, making it go this way, then that way around her legs.

'Look, Mummy! It's so pretty! Can I have it?'

Sydney smiled as she pulled out outfit after outfit. A mermaid tail, another princess dress, this time in pink, a Halloween costume festooned with layers and layers of black and orange netting. Sydney hesitated as she dipped into the box and pulled out a onesie made of brown fur. It had a long tail, and ears on the hood. Sydney pressed it to her nose and inhaled, closing her eyes as tears leaked from the corners of them.

Olivia had loved this onesie. She'd used to sleep in it. She'd been wearing it when… The memory came bursting to the fore.

The morning I found you.

She smiled bravely as she inhaled the scent

of the onesie once again. It had been washed, but she was convinced it still had her daughter's scent.

An image of that awful morning filled her head. The day before Olivia had said she had a headache. She hadn't wanted to go to school. But Sydney had had a long day of surgeries, and Alastair had had work, so they'd needed their daughter to go in.

At the end of the day, when Sydney had gone to pick her up, Olivia had seemed in a very low mood—not her normal self. When they'd got home she'd said she was tired and that her head still hurt, so Sydney had given her some medicine and a drink and told her she could go to bed. She'd kept checking on her, but her daughter had been sleeping, so she'd just put it down to some virus.

When Alastair had got home he'd been celebrating a success at work, and that night they'd gone to bed and made love. The next morning Alastair had left early. Sydney had called for Olivia to come down for breakfast but she hadn't answered. So she'd gone up to get her and instantly known something was wrong. The second she'd walked into her daughter's bedroom.

She'd not been able to wake her. She'd called her name, shaken her shoulders—nothing. Olivia had been hot, and Sydney had gone to unzip the onesie, and that was when she'd seen the rash and called 999.

Sydney laid the onesie down. This was the last thing that Olivia had worn. It was too sad to focus on. Too painful.

She dug further into the box and pulled out a pirate costume.

Now, this has a happier memory!

There'd been a World Book Day and all the school's children had been asked to come in as one of their favourite characters. At the time Olivia had been into pirate stories, but none of the characters had been girl pirates, so she'd decided that she would be a pirate anyway. Sydney had rolled up a pair of blue jeans to Olivia's calves, bought a red and white striped tee shirt and a tricorne hat, and used an eye patch that they'd been gifted in an old party bag.

Olivia had spent all day answering every question Sydney had asked her with, *'Arr!'* and, *'Aye, Captain!'*

Sydney laughed at the memory, her heart swelling with warmth and feeling once again. Seeing her daughter happy in her mind's eye, hearing that chuckle, seeing her smile, feeling her—

She stopped.

Oh... Could Nathan be right? That I need to focus on the days she lived?

No. No, he couldn't be right. He hadn't experienced grief like this—he didn't know what he was talking about.

But I do feel good when I remember the good times...

Perhaps holding on to the grief, on to the day she died, on to the *pain* was the thing that anchored Sydney in the past? Maybe she was holding herself back? Isolating herself so that she could wallow in her daughter's memory. Was that why Alastair had moved on? Had he been able to let go of the misery and instead chosen to remember his daughter's vibrant life, not just her death?

Stunned, she sat there for a moment, holding

the pirate tee shirt and wondering. Her gaze travelled to the other boxes. Books. Toys. Clothes. Was holding on to her daughter like this the thing that was keeping her from moving on? Perhaps keeping her daughter's things in the attic had kept Olivia trapped in a place that tortured them both.

I know I have to try to move on...but by letting go of my past will I lose my daughter?

The thought that maybe she ought to donate some of Olivia's stuff to a charity shop entered her head, and she immediately stood up straight and stared down at the open box.

Give her things away?

No. Surely not. If she gave Olivia's things away, how on earth would she remember her?

You've remembered her just fine with all this stuff packed away in the attic for four years...

She let out a breath. Then another. Steadier. It calmed her racing heart. What if she didn't do it all in one go? What if she just gave away a few pieces? Bit by bit? It might be easier that way. She'd keep the stuff that mattered, though. The onesie. Olivia's favourite toys—her doll and her teddy bear Baxter. Maybe one or two of her daughter's favourite books. The last one they'd been reading, for sure.

Maybe...

She saw the look on Nathan's face as he'd left. *'I'm sorry I upset you...'*

I need to apologise.

Guilt filled her and she suddenly felt sick. Gripping her stomach, she sat down and clutched the onesie for strength. For inspiration.

She would have to apologise. Make it up to him. Explain.

If he even wants to listen.

But then she thought, *He will listen.* He was a doctor. He was good at that. And she needed to let him know that she cared.

As she thought of how she could make it up to him she saw some other boxes, further towards the back of the attic. She frowned, wondering what they were, and, crouching, she shuffled over to them, tore off the tape and opened them up.

Christmas decorations.

Perhaps she could show Nathan in more than one way that she was trying to make things right...

She'd used to love Christmas. Olivia had *adored* it. What child didn't? It was a season of great fun and great food, rounded off with a day full of presents.

She particularly remembered the Christmas before Olivia had died. She'd asked for a bike and Sydney and Alastair had found her a sparkly pink one, with tassels on the handlebars and a basket on the front adorned with plastic flowers.

Olivia had spent all that Christmas Day peddling up and down on the pathways and around the back garden, her little knees going up and down, biting her bottom lip as she concentrated on her coordination. And then later that day, after they'd all eaten their dinner, pulled crackers, told each other bad jokes and were sitting curled up on the sofa together, Olivia had asked if next Christmas she could have a little brother or sister.

Sydney's gaze alighted on the bike, covered by an old brown blanket...

She swallowed the lump in her throat. Olivia would have loved a sibling. A little baby to play with. What would she have made of Anna? No doubt the girls would have been best friends.

Thinking of Anna made her think of Nathan. She was so very grateful for him coming over today. Offering his olive branch. He had given her a new way of thinking. And how had she reacted? Badly! She'd seen it as an attack on her rather than seeing the kind and caring motivation behind it.

She could see now what he'd been trying to say. And she had missed it completely. It was true. She had been focusing so much on her daughter's death that she had forgotten to focus on her daughter's life.

And Nathan had also told her about his MS. It had been so brave of him to share that with her, and it must have been troubling him for some time. It must have been why he'd been so ill that day she'd looked after Anna. And hadn't Anna said her daddy was always sick and tired?

Poor Nathan. But at least he knew what he was fighting. It had a name. It had a treatment plan. She would have to look it up online and see what relapsing remitting multiple sclerosis really was. Especially if—as she was starting to hope—they were going to be involved with each other. It would be good to know what to expect and how to help.

Nathan had given her a gift. A way to try and lift the burden that she'd been feeling all this time. The guilt. The grief. He'd given her something else to think about. Told her to try and remember Olivia in a different way. A less heart-breaking way.

Could she do it?

Maybe she could start by honouring the season...

Sydney lifted up a box of decorations and began to make her way back down the ladder.

CHAPTER SEVEN

MRS COURTAULD HAD arrived for her appointment. She was there for a blood pressure check, and though she could have made an appointment to see the practice nurse to get it done she'd deliberately made a doctor's appointment to see Nathan.

She came into his room, shuffling her feet, and settled down into a chair with a small groan.

He forced a smile. 'Mrs Courtauld…how are you?'

'Oh, I'm good, Doctor, thank you. I must say *you* look a bit glum. I've been round the block enough times to know when someone's *pretending* to be okay.'

He laughed. 'I'm sorry. I'll try to do better. Are you ready for Christmas?'

Sydney's rejection of him had hurt terribly. Although he didn't think she'd rejected him because of his health—unlike Gwyneth—the way she'd thrown him out still stung.

'Of course I am! Not that there's much preparation for me to do…not with my Alfred gone, God rest his soul. But my son is going to pick me up on Christmas Eve and I'm going to his house to spend the season.'

'Sounds great. Let someone else look after you and do all the work. Why not?'

'I've brought those things that you asked for.' She reached down into her shopping trolley and pulled out a small packet wrapped in a brown paper bag and passed it across the table to him. 'I asked around and so many people wanted to help. I hope it's the kind of thing you were after. Surprisingly, there was quite a bit that people had.'

He peeked inside and smiled. It *was* rather a lot. More than he could have hoped for. But would it be any good now?

'Perfect. Thank you, Mrs C. I appreciate all the trouble you went to to coordinate this. Now, shall we check your blood pressure?'

She began to remove her coat. 'Anything for

our Sydney.' She looked at him slyly. 'Will you be spending Christmas together, then?'

He felt his face colour, but smiled anyway, even though he suspected that the chance of his spending Christmas with Sydney had about the same odds as his MS disappearing without trace. Choosing not to answer, he wheeled his chair over to his patient.

Mrs Courtauld couldn't know that they'd had a falling out. He'd been trying to help Sydney, but maybe it had come out wrong? He'd been going over and over what he'd said, trying to remember the *way* he'd said it as well as *what* he'd said, and he'd got angry at himself.

His patient rolled up her sleeve, staring at him, assessing him. 'She deserves some happiness, young Sydney. She's had her sadness, and she's paid her dues in that respect. Enough grief to last a thousand lifetimes. It's her turn to be happy.' She looked up at him and made him meet her gaze. 'And you could do that for her, Doctor. You and that little girl of yours.'

'Thanks, Mrs C.'

'Call me Elizabeth.'

He smiled and checked her blood pressure.

* * *

A bell rang overhead as Sydney walked into the charity shop. There was only one in Silverdale, and sales from it aided the local hospice. She hadn't been in for a long time, but was reassured to see a familiar face behind the counter.

'Syd! Long time, no see! How are you?'

Sydney made her way to the counter with her two bags of clothes. It wasn't much. But it was a start. 'Oh, you know. Ambling on with life.'

'We've missed seeing you in here. We could always rely on you to come in most weekends, looking for a new book or two.'

'I'm sorry it's been a while.' She paused for a moment. She could back out if she wanted to. She didn't have to hand these items over. 'I've... er...brought in a few things. Children's clothes.'

'Children's...? Oh, wait...not *Olivia's*?'

Her cheeks flushed with heat and she nodded. 'Just one or two outfits. Thought I'd better start sorting, you know.'

Lisa nodded sadly. 'Sometimes it's what we need to do, to move forward.'

She didn't want to cry. Wasn't that what Nathan

had said in a roundabout way? And look at how she had treated him for it! Perhaps everyone had been thinking the same, but she'd been the only one not to know.

'It's all been laundered and pressed. You should be able to put it straight out.' She placed the two bags on the counter and Lisa peered inside, her fingers touching the fabric of a skirt that Olivia had worn only once, because she'd been going through a growth spurt.

'That's grand, Syd. I'll have a sort through and maybe make a window display with them. Launch them with style, eh?'

Unable to speak, Sydney nodded. Then, blinking back tears, she hurriedly left the shop.

Outside in the cold air she began to breathe again, sucking in great lungsful of the crisp air and strangely feeling a part of her burden begin to lift.

It had been a difficult thing to do, but she'd done it. She'd made a start. Hopefully next time it would be easier. But doing it in little instalments was better than trying to get rid of it all in one go. She knew that wasn't the way for her. Slow and steady would win this race.

But now she had a really hard thing to do. She had to see Nathan. Apologise. There was one last committee meeting tonight and perhaps there, on neutral ground, she could let him know that she'd been in the wrong. That it would be nice if he could forgive her. But if not…

She dreaded to think of *if not*…

Those hours in the attic—those hours spent sorting her daughter's clothes for donation—had made her begin to see just how much she had begun to enjoy and even to depend upon Nathan's friendship.

She'd been a fool to react so badly.

She could only hope he would forgive her in a way Alastair had never been able to.

It was the last committee meeting before the big day. The Christmas market and nativity—and the anniversary of Olivia's death—were just two days away, and this was their last chance to make sure that everything was spick and span and organised correctly. That there were no last-minute hiccups.

There was palpable excitement in the room, and Miriam had even gone to the trouble to supply them with chocolate biscuits to help fuel their discussion.

Sydney sat nervously at one end of the table, far from Nathan, anxious to get the opportunity to talk to him and put things right. Her mind buzzed with all the things she needed to say. Wanted to say. She'd hoped she'd have a chance to talk to him before the meeting started, but he'd come in late once again and grabbed his place at the table without looking at her.

'The marquees are all organised and will be delivered tomorrow and erected on-site. Items for the tombola are all sorted, and Mike has promised us the use of his PA and sound system this year.' Miriam beamed.

'How are we doing regarding the food stalls? Sydney?'

She perked up at the sound of her name and riffled through her notes, her hands shaking. 'The WI ladies in the village are in full cake-making mode and most will bring their cakes down in the morning for arrangement. The manageress of The Tea-Total Café has promised us a gingerbread spectacular, whatever that may be.'

'Sounds intriguing. Any entries this year for the Best Pet competition?'

She nodded. 'The usual suspects. I'm sure Jim will be hoping to win back the trophy from Gerry this year.' She smiled, hoping Nathan would look at her so she could catch his eye, but he just kept gazing down at his own notes.

She could almost feel her heart breaking. Had she hurt him so much with her words the other day that he couldn't even *look* at her now? Was she shut out of his world completely? It hurt to think so.

But then he looked up, glanced at her. 'Can I enter Lottie?'

She turned to him and smiled hopefully. 'You can.'

Though they were seated two chairs apart, she itched to reach for his hand across the table. To squeeze his fingers. Let him know that she was sorry. That she hadn't meant what she'd said. That she'd had a knee-jerk reaction because she was frightened of letting go.

But then he looked away again as he scribbled something into his notes.

Her heart sank.

Malcolm filled them in on what was happening with the beer tent, the businesses that had applied to have a stall and sell their wares, who'd be covering first aid and said that licences for closing the road to the council had been approved.

'All that's left that's out of our hands is the nativity. Dr Jones, I believe your daughter is going to be the star attraction this year? Any idea how rehearsals are going?'

'Miss Howarth and Anna assure me that it's all going very well.'

'And I've arranged a small area for the donkey and other farm animals to be kept in whilst they're not performing,' added Sydney, hoping to join in on his contribution.

'Excellent, excellent!' Malcolm enthused.

Once the meeting was over Sydney quickly gathered her things and hurried out into the cold after Nathan. She *had* to catch up with him. She couldn't just let him go. Not like this.

The village had already gone full-force on Christmas decorations. The main street was adorned with fairy lights, criss-crossing from one side to the other, so as people walked along at night it was like being in a sparkly tunnel. Trees were lit and shining bright from people's homes, and some residents had really gone to town, decorating their gardens and trees into small grottos. It didn't hurt her any more to see it.

'Nathan!'

He turned, and when he saw her his face darkened. She saw him glance at the floor.

Standing in front of him, she waited until he looked up and met her gaze. 'Thank you for waiting. I…er…really need to apologise to you. For how I reacted—well, *overreacted* to what you said.'

He stood staring at her, saying nothing.

'I was so in the wrong. I wasn't ready to hear what you said, and I thought you were telling me I needed to be over Olivia's death, and…you weren't. You were telling me to focus on the good times and not the bad, and that was something completely different to saying, *Get over it Sydney!*'

She was wringing her hands, over and over.

'You were trying to help me. Trying to make me see that if I could just try and look at it in another way then it needn't be so painful. So sad. That it was trapping me in the past—'

He reached out and steadied her hands, holding them in his. 'It's okay.'

Relieved that he was talking to her, she had to apologise even more. 'It's not. I behaved abominably. I kicked you out of my house! You *and* Anna! I feel so terrible about that…so inhuman and abysmal and—'

He silenced her with a kiss.

It was so unexpected. One moment she was pouring her heart out, blurting out her apologies, her regrets for her mistake, hoping he would understand, hoping he would forgive her, and the next his lips were on hers. His glorious lips! Warm and tender and so, so forgiving…

She could have cried. The beginnings of tears stung her eyes at first, but then ebbed away as the wondrousness of their kiss continued.

He cradled her face in his hands as he kissed her and he breathed her in. Sydney moaned—a small noise in the back of her throat as she sank against him. This was…amazing! This was what they could have had the other day if he hadn't thought otherwise and backed off. What they could have had if only she hadn't got angry or scared or whatever it was she had been, so that tricks were playing in her head.

Why had they delayed doing this? They fitted so perfectly!

His tongue was searching out hers as he kissed her deeper and deeper. She almost couldn't breathe. She'd forgotten how to. All she knew right now was that she was so happy he'd forgiven her. He must have done. Or surely he wouldn't be kissing her like this.

And just when she thought she was seeing stars, and that her lungs were about to burst, he broke away from her and stared deeply into her eyes.

She gazed back into his and saw a depth of raw emotion there, a passion that could no longer be bridled. He wanted her.

And she him.

'Drive me home,' she said.

He nodded once and they got into the car.

It didn't take them long to reach her bedroom. Once inside, their giggles faded fast as they stood for a moment, just looking at each other.

Had she ever needed to be with a man this much?

Sydney needed to touch him. Needed to feel

his hands upon her. She knew that he would not make the first move unless she showed him that this was what she wanted.

She reached up and, keeping eye contact, began to undo the buttons of his shirt.

He sucked in a breath. 'Sydney...'

'I need you, Nathan.' She pulled his shirt out from his trousers and then her hands found his belt buckle.

Nathan's mouth came down to claim hers, his tongue delicately arousing as he licked and tasted her lips.

She pulled his belt free and tossed it to the floor. She undid the button, unzipped the zipper, and as his trousers fell to the floor he stepped out of them and removed his shirt.

'Now me,' she urged him.

She felt his hands take the hem of her jumper and lift it effortlessly over her head, and then he did the same with her tee shirt, his eyes darkening with desire as her long dark hair spread over her milky-white shoulders. His hands cupped her breasts, his thumbs drifting over her nipples through the lace, and she groaned, arching her back so that her breasts pressed into his hands.

His mouth found her neck, her shoulders, her collarbone, all the while causing sensations on her skin that she had not experienced for a very long time, awakening her body, making her crave his every touch.

He undid her jeans, sliding them down her long legs. His lips kissed their way down her thighs and then came slowly back up to find the lace of her underwear. Then he was breathing in her scent and kissing her once again through the lace.

She almost lost it.

When had she *ever* felt this naked? This vulnerable? And yet...she revelled in it. Gloried in it. She knew she needed to show him her vulnerability, show that despite that she still wanted to be with him. To trust him. After the way she'd treated him the other day, she needed him to know that she couldn't be without him.

'You're so beautiful...' he breathed, and the heat of his breath sent goosebumps along her skin.

His hands were at her sides, going round to her back. He found the clip on her bra and undid it. She shrugged it off easily, groaning at the feel of his hands cupping her breasts, properly this time, at the feel of his mouth, his kisses.

'Nathan...'

She could feel his arousal, hard against her, and she unhooked his boxers, sliding them to the floor.

As he lay back on the bed she looked at him in triumph. This beautiful, magnificent man was all hers. And she'd so very nearly cast him aside!

She groaned as she thought of what she might have lost and lay beside him, wrapping her limbs around him so that they were entwined as their mouths joined together once more.

All he'd ever done was listen to her. Understand her. Give her space and time to be ready to talk to him. Where else would she find a man that patient? That understanding and empathetic?

He rolled her under him and breathed her name as his hands roamed her body, creating sensations that she had forgotten she'd ever felt before. She needed him so much. Longed to be *part* of him.

She pulled him closer, urging him on as he began to make love to her.

This was what life was about! Really living. Being a *part* of life—not merely existing. It was about celebrating a relationship, sharing fears and desires and finding that one person you could do that with. About opening up to another person and being okay about that.

Nathan had shared his own vulnerability, his multiple sclerosis. It must have taken him a great deal of courage. And he had shared Anna with her. Letting her get to know his daughter. He couldn't have known that they would get on like this. Must have been worried that Sydney might reject them both once she got to know them.

I nearly did.

She suddenly understood how much pain he must have felt when she'd kicked him out and she pulled him to her once more, hoping as he cried out and gripped the headboard that he would finally see just how much he'd been right to trust her, after all.

She wrapped him safely in her arms and held on tight.

Afterwards, they lay in bed in each other's arms.

Sydney's head was resting in the crook of Nathan's shoulder and he lay there, lazily stroking the skin on her arms. 'I really missed you, you know...'

She turned and kissed his chest. 'I missed you, too. I hated what I did.'

'I understood. You were lashing out because what I said hurt you. You thought I was asking you to give up even *thinking* about your daughter.' He planted a kiss on the top of her head. 'I gave you the advice someone gave me once.'

She turned, laying her chin upon his chest and staring up into his face. 'What do you mean?'

'When I got my diagnosis I was in complete shock. It was like I was mourning my old life. The life in which I could do anything whenever I wanted, without having to think about muscle weakness or spasms or taking medication every day. I mourned the body that I thought would slowly deteriorate until it was useless, and I couldn't get over that.'

'What happened?'

'Anna was born. I was euphoric about that. But then I started thinking about all the ways I might let her down as a father. What if I missed school shows, or parents' evenings, or birthdays...? And then Gwyneth left, totally appalled by the fact that she'd got involved with someone with this illness, and that made me feel under even more pressure from myself. I *couldn't* let Anna down! She only had me to rely on. I *had* to be well. I *had* to be positive. But something kept pulling me back towards feeling sorry for myself. I'd lost my partner and my health and I couldn't get past that.'

She kissed his chest. 'I'm so sorry.'

'I went to a counselling group. It was led by a really good therapist. She helped me see that I was mourning a loss. I was mourning my future. She told me to look at it in a different way. Not to focus on what I'd lost, but on what I'd gained. I didn't necessarily have a bad life in front of me, that—I had a beautiful baby daughter who loved me unconditionally and I knew what my limits might be. But they weren't necessarily there. I had to celebrate the new me rather than mourn the old me. Does that make sense?'

She nodded, laying her head back down against his beautifully strong chest. 'It does.'

'Gwyneth leaving wasn't about me. It was about

her and what *she* could deal with. I couldn't control her reaction, but I could control mine. And that's why I decided to focus on the good that was coming. On what I could learn about myself in the process. Discovering hidden depths of strength.'

'Did you find them?'

'Oh, yes!' He laughed, squeezing her to him. Then he paused for a moment and rolled above her, staring deeply into her grey eyes. 'Have you?'

She nodded silently, feeling tears of joy welling in her eyes.

'I think I'm starting to. Because of you.'

He smiled and kissed her.

CHAPTER EIGHT

IT WAS THE afternoon of the Christmas market and nativity and Anna was incredibly excited.

Nathan hadn't been able to get in touch with Sydney yesterday, being busy at work, but at least now he felt better about the direction they were heading in.

It was all going well.

When she'd slammed the door on the two of them and he'd had to walk away it had been the hardest thing he had ever done. Even harder still was the fact that Anna had been full of chatter about the kittens. When could she go and visit them again? Would Sydney mind if they went round every day?

He'd managed to distract her by getting her to read through her lines for her part in the nativity, and he'd been grateful when she'd gone quiet in the back of the car as she read her little script.

But now…? Everything was going well for them. He hoped he would get a moment to talk to Sydney, because he knew that this day would be hard for her.

She'd told him it was the anniversary of Olivia's death. That she'd always faced this day alone in the past. He tried for a moment to imagine what it would be like if he was mourning Anna, but it was too dreadful. He dashed the thought away instantly.

There was so much to do. He'd promised to help out with setting up the marquees and organising the stands, and said he'd be a general dogs-body for anyone who needed him.

Surely Sydney would be there too. She had stalls to organise. The Best Pet show to judge. He hoped he'd get a moment to talk to her, to make sure she was okay.

He parked in the pub car park and walked down to the square that already looked as if it was heaving with people and noise. Right now it seemed like chaos, but he hoped that by the afternoon, and for the nativity in the evening, it would all run smoothly and everyone would be entertained.

He searched for Sydney's familiar long chocolate hair in the crowd, but he couldn't see her amongst all the people bustling about.

This was his and Anna's first Christmas in Silverdale, and he was looking forward to making new connections with people that he'd only ever met as patients. He wanted to let people see him as someone other than a doctor. To let them see that he was a father. A neighbour. A friend.

Tonight was going to go really well. He knew it. And hopefully some of the villagers who didn't know him yet would get the opportunity to meet him and welcome him as a valued member of their community.

'Dr Jones! How good to see you. Are you doing anything at the moment?'

Nathan noticed Miriam, the secretary of the committee, loitering within an empty marquee that had tables set up but nothing else. 'No. How can I help?'

'I'm running the tombola, and all the donated items are in boxes in the van, but I can't lift them with my arthritis. Would you be able to?'

He smiled. This he could do. He was a strong

man. He could lift and carry whatever she asked of him and he would do it. 'A pleasure, Miriam. Where's the van?'

Miriam pointed at a white van parked on the edge of the barriers. 'You are a dear. A real bonus to our committee. We needed some new blood!'

He waved away her compliment. 'I'm sure Dr Preston is hugely missed. I just hope I can fill his shoes.'

Miriam beamed at him. 'You far surpass Richard Preston already, Dr Jones, just by my looking at you!'

Nathan grinned. 'If I was thirty years older, Miriam…'

'Thirty? Oh, you're too kind! *Much* too kind!'

Nathan headed to her van, opened it up and started pulling out boxes. Some were very light, and he assumed they were full of teddy bears and the like. But others were considerably heavier and he struggled to carry one or two.

Whatever were people giving away—boulders?

He lugged the boxes over to the marquee, and just as he set down the last one he heard Sydney's laugh.

Instantly his heart began to pound. She was *laughing*. She was *here*. She was helping out. Same as him. Just as she'd promised she would.

He looked about for her, and once he'd made sure Miriam was okay to empty out the boxes by herself found himself heading over to the pen that Sydney was building along with Mr Bradley from Wicklegate Farm—the owner of Bert the donkey.

'Sydney!'

She turned at the sound of his voice. 'Nathan!'

He kissed her on the lips in greeting—a gesture that earned a wry smile from Mr Bradley.

'How are you doing? I meant to call you earlier—'

'I'm fine!' she answered brightly.

'Really? You don't have to pretend. I know today must be difficult for you. I thought that—'

'Nathan… Honestly. I'm doing great.'

He tried to see if she was just being brave for him, but he couldn't see any deception in her eyes. Perhaps she *was* doing okay? He stood back as she continued to build the pen, fastening some nuts on the final fence with a spanner.

'It's for Bert and the goats and things. What do you think?'

'Erm…I'm no expert on animal holding pens, but these look good to me.'

She kissed him on the cheek. 'I've got lots to do. Off you go! I know you're busy, too. You don't have to hold my hand. I'm doing okay. I've got through this day before.'

He stilled her hands. 'You were on your own before.'

'And I'm not now. I promise if I have a problem, or get upset, I'll come and find you.'

'If you're sure…?'

'I'm sure.' She smiled at him. 'I appreciate your concern. Oh, I almost forgot—I have Olivia's costume for Anna.' She stepped out of the pen and over to her car, opening the boot and bringing back a small bag. 'It should fit. It's all loose robes, and she can tie it tighter with the belt.'

He nodded, accepting the bag. 'Thanks. She nearly had to wear what I'd made her.'

He would just have to trust her. She knew he would be in her corner if she needed him.

'I'm around. Just give me a shout and maybe we can grab a snack later? Before it all kicks off?'

She blew him a kiss. 'I'll come and find you.'

'I'll hold you to it.' He smiled and waved, and then, tearing himself away, headed off to deliver the costume to his daughter.

Sydney did as she'd promised. A few hours later, when the market was all set up and ready to open to the public, she sought out Nathan, She found him at the bakery tent, manhandling a giant gingerbread grotto scene to place it on a table, and they headed off to sit on the steps around the village Christmas tree.

Nathan paid for a couple of cups of tea for them both and then joined her, wrapping his arm around her shoulders in the cold evening air.

The Christmas market looked picture-postcard-perfect. The marquees were all bedecked with Christmas lighting, carols were being played over the PA system in readiness and—oh, the aromas! The scent of hot dogs, fried onions, candy floss, roasting chestnuts, gingerbread and freshly brewed coffee floated in the air, causing their mouths to water.

'Looks amazing, doesn't it?' she said, looking out at all their hard work. It felt good to be appreciating—finally—the magic of Christmas once again.

'It certainly does. Worth all those meetings we had to sit through.'

She laughed. 'When it all comes together like this it's hard to believe we managed to achieve it.' She paused. 'Did you get the costume to Anna? Did it fit?'

He nodded. 'Perfectly. Thank you.'

They sat in companionable silence for a while, sipping their tea and just enjoying the sensation of *being*. Enjoying the moment. It was nice to sit there together, watching everyone else beavering away.

Nathan took her hand in his and smiled at her as she snuggled into his arms. But then she sat forward, peering into the distance.

'Look! They're letting everyone in. Come on—we have stations to man!' She tossed her paper teacup into a nearby bin and headed off to her first job of the evening.

Nathan watched her go.

Was she really as unaffected by this day as she seemed?

He doubted it.

Frowning, he followed after her.

Silverdale was brimming with activity and the centre of the high street looked amazing. Sydney would have liked to truly immerse herself in the marvel of the beautiful fairy lights everywhere. To listen to the carol singers and their music. To taste the wonderfully aromatic food on display and talk to all the visitors and customers. Enjoy the floral displays.

But she couldn't.

She knew she had work to do, but she was beginning to feel guilty.

Was she really pretending that today wasn't *the day*? Had she deliberately tried to ignore it because she already knew how guilty she now felt? She hadn't mourned as much. She hadn't *remembered* her daughter the way she usually did today.

She felt bad—even if *'usually'* mostly involved staring at photographs all day and often ended with her being a crumpled, sobbing heap.

Her heart felt pained. Just breathing seemed to be exhausting. And yet she had to keep up a steady stream of false smiles and fake jollity for everyone she met or saw.

Was she lying to Nathan? Or to herself?

The stallholders were doing lively business, and she could see money changing hands wherever she looked. People she knew walked their dogs, or pushed buggies, or stood arm in arm looking in wonder and awe at their hard-worked-for Christmas Market. And now crowds were gathering at the main stage for the crowning glory of the evening—the nativity play.

She wandered through the tent with her clipboard, viewing the animals entered for the Best Pet competition. Their owners stood by, looking at her hopefully as she met each one, asked a little about their animal, remembering to remark on their colouring or lovely temperament and scribbling her thoughts on paper.

But she was doing it on automatic pilot.

Until she got to a black rabbit.

Lottie.

Lottie sat in her cage quite calmly, oblivious to all the hubbub going on around her. Her eye had healed quite well, and apart from a slight grey glaze to it no one would be able to guess that she had been attacked and almost blinded.

Sydney stared at the rabbit, her pen poised over her score sheet, remembering the first time Nathan had brought Lottie to her. How hard it had been to fight her feelings for him. How she'd tried to tell herself to stay away from him and not get involved. She hadn't listened to herself. He'd wormed his way into her affections somehow, with those cheeky twinkling eyes of his— *and, my goodness, it had felt so good to lie in his arms. Protected. Coveted. Cherished.*

And he was making her forget. Wasn't he?

No! Not forget. Just deal with it in a different way.

Losing Olivia had hurt like nothing she could ever have imagined. One minute her daughter had been lively, full of life, giggling and happy, and the next she'd wound up in a hospital bed, and Sydney had sat by her bedside for every moment, hoping for a miracle.

She'd felt so helpless. A mother was meant to protect her children—but how on earth were you meant to defend them against things you couldn't see? Bacteria. Viruses. Contagion. They were all sneaky. Taking hold of young, healthy, vital bodies and tearing them asunder. All she'd been able to do was sit. And pray. And talk to her daughter who could no longer hear her. Beg her to fight. Beg her to hold on for a little while longer.

It had all been useless.

She felt a bit sick.

What am I doing here?

'We need the result, Sydney. The nativity is about to start.'

Sydney nodded to Malcolm absently. She wanted to see the nativity. She'd promised Anna she would watch her and cheer her on as she rode in on Bert.

She marked a score for Lottie and then passed her results to Malcolm, who took them over to his small stand in the tent.

Pet owners gathered anxiously—all of them

smiling, all of them hopeful for a win. There were some lovely animals, from little mice to Fletcher the Great Dane. Fletcher was a big, lolloping giant of a dog, with the sweetest nature.

Malcolm cleared his throat. 'In third place, with six points, we have Montgomery! A gorgeous example of a golden Syrian hamster.'

Everyone applauded as a little girl stepped forward to receive a purple ribbon for Montgomery.

'In second place, with eight points, we have Jonesy—a beautiful ginger tom.'

Again there was applause, and a young boy came forward to collect his ribbon.

'And in first place, with ten points, we have Lottie the rabbit!'

There were more cheers. More applause.

'Lottie's owner can't be here to collect her prize as she's preparing for her role in the nativity. So perhaps our judge—our fabulous Silverdale veterinary surgeon—would like to give us a few words as to why Lottie has won tonight's contest? Everyone...I give you Sydney Harper!'

Reluctantly, Sydney stepped over to address the crowd—a sea of faces of people she recognised. People she knew from many years of living in this community. There was Miss Howarth, Olivia's schoolteacher. And Cara the lollipop lady, who'd used to help Olivia cross the road outside school. Mr Franklin, who would always talk to Olivia as they walked to school each morning...

'Thank you, Mr Speaker.'

She tried to gather her thoughts as she stood at the microphone. She'd been in a daze for a while. Now it was time to focus. Time to ignore the sickness she could feel building in her stomach.

'There were some amazing entries in this year's competition, and it was great to see such a broad variety of much-loved animals, who all looked fantastic, I'm sure you agree.'

She paused to force a smile.

'I was looking for a certain something this year. I have the honour of knowing a lot of these animals personally. I think I can honestly say I've seen most of them in my surgery, so I know a little about them all. But Lottie won my vote this year because... Well...she's been through a lot. She went through a difficult time and almost lost her life. Instead she lost her eye, but despite that…despite the horror that she has experienced this year, she has stayed strong.'

Her gaze fell upon Nathan, who had appeared at the back of the crowd.

'She fought. And tonight, when I saw her in her cage, looking beautiful in her shiny black coat and with a quiet dignity, I knew I had found my winner. Prizes shouldn't always go to the most attractive, or the most well-behaved, or the most well-groomed. Animals, like people, are more than just their looks. There's something beneath that. A character. A *strength*. And Lottie has that—in bucketloads.'

She nodded and stepped back, indicating that she had finished.

Malcolm led the applause, thanked her, and then urged everyone to make their way to the main stage for the nativity.

Sydney waited for the main crowd to go, and when there was a clearing she walked out of the marquee, feeling a little light-headed.

She felt a hand on her arm. 'Thank you.'

Nathan.

'Oh…it was nothing.'

'Anna will be thrilled Lottie won. She didn't want to miss it, but she's getting ready for the show.'

'Make sure you collect your voucher from Malcolm later.'

'I will.'

'Right. Well…' She wanted to head for the stage. But it seemed Nathan still had something to say.

'You know, you were right just then.'

'Oh…?'

'About people having depths that you can't see. You know, you're a lot like that little rabbit. You have that inner strength.'

She didn't feel like it right now. 'We…er…we need to get going.'

'Wait!' He pulled something from behind his back. 'I got you this.'

He handed over a small parcel, wrapped in shiny paper and tied with an elaborate bow.

'It's for Christmas. Obviously.' He smiled at her. 'But I thought it was important to give it to you today.'

'What is it?'

He laughed. 'I can't tell you that! It's a surprise. Hopefully…a good one. Merry Christmas.'

Suddenly felt this was wrong. Much too wrong! She shouldn't be getting *presents*. Not *today*.

Nathan was wrong.

Today was the worst day to give her his gift.

'I…I don't know what to say.'

'I believe thank you is traditional.'

He smiled and went to kiss her, but she backed off.

'I can't do this,' she muttered.

'Syd? What's the—?'

'You shouldn't give me a gift. Not today. A present? Today? You know what this day is. You know what it means.'

'Of course! Which is why I wanted to give it to you now. To celebrate you moving forward, to give you an incentive to—'

It was too much. Sydney couldn't stand there a moment longer. She had to get away. She had to leave. She—

I promised Anna I'd watch her in the nativity.

Torn, she stood rooted to the spot, angst tearing

its way through her as grief and guilt flooded in. This was *not* the way she should be on the anniversary of her daughter's death! She ought to be showing respect. She ought to be remembering her daughter. *Olivia.* Not Anna. Or Nathan. They couldn't be Olivia's replacements. They could never be what her daughter had been to her. Or mean as much.

Could they?

Her heart told her they might, even as the agony of this indecision almost made her cry out.

'Syd…?'

'Nathan, please don't! I can't do this. I can't be with you—'

'Sydney—'

'It's over. Nathan? Do you hear me? I'm done.'

He let go of her arms and stepped back from her as if she'd just slapped him.

She'd never felt more alone.

Nathan just stood there, looking at her, sadness and hurt in his eyes.

'You should remember what you said about Lottie. You're strong, too, you know… You've been through something…*unimaginable* and you're still here. But if you can't see it in your-self…if you can't feel it…believe it…then I need to keep my distance, too. I need to think about Anna. I can't mess her around. If you can't com-mit to us the way I need you to—'

'I never wanted to hurt you or Anna.'

'I know.' He looked away at the happy crowds. 'But…you did. Please let Anna see you before you leave.'

And he walked away.

Sydney gulped back a grief-racked sob, won-dering what the hell she'd just done.

Sydney stood at the front of the crowd, waiting for Anna's big moment. She'd split up from Na-than as he'd headed backstage to give his daugh-ter one last pep talk.

Guilt and shame were filling her. Today was the anniversary of her daughter's death. And she'd kept busy—tried her hardest not to think about her. She hadn't even gone to the cemetery to put down some flowers for her. She hadn't been for so long. Who knew what her daughter's grave looked like now? Mrs C had laid a flower there in November—was it still there? Dead and brittle? Covered by fallen leaves or weeds?

And she was here, waiting to applaud another little girl. What was she *doing*? She'd even given Anna Olivia's old costume. She'd be riding Bert, too. Saying the same lines. It would be too much to bear.

And now she'd hurt Nathan. Played around with that man's heart because she hadn't known whether she was ready to accept it completely.

Feeling sick, she was about to turn and push her way through the crowds when she noticed Bert the donkey come into view, with Anna perched proudly on his back.

Sydney gasped. She'd been expecting to be tormented with memories. But it was *so* clear now. Anna was *nothing* like Olivia. The shape of her face was different. She had her father's jawline, her father's eyes.

If I'd continued with Nathan I wouldn't have been just taking him on, but Anna, too. I'd have let them both down. And now I've broken his heart, and Anna's too...

Overwhelmed by shock and guilt, Sydney stood

silently and watched. Suddenly she was smiling with encouragement as Anna's gaze met her own. She felt so proud of Anna. Almost as proud of her as she had been of Olivia, doing the same thing.

How can that be?

As she watched the little girl ride Bert over to his mark by the hay bale, dismount and then take the hand of her Joseph, Sydney felt sadness seize her once more. She could recall Olivia doing that very thing. She'd taken Joseph's hand and been led into the stable too.

'And Joseph and Mary could find nowhere to stay. The only place left to them was with the animals in the stable. And in the place where lambs were born Mary gave birth to baby Jesus...' A small boy at the side of the stage intoned his words into a microphone.

Anna reappeared, this time without her pregnancy bump and holding a doll, swaddled in a thick white blanket, which she lay down into a manger.

Why am I crying?

Sydney blinked a few times and dabbed at her eyes with the back of her hand. Was she being like the innkeeper of Bethlehem? Telling Nathan and Anna there was no room for them in her home? Her heart?

She'd felt there *was* room. It had been there. She'd felt it. Even now she could feel it.

Sydney turned and pushed her way through the crowds, tears streaming freely down her face, unable to look. Unable to face the future she would have had if she'd stayed with Nathan. Unable to believe that she had that inner strength Nathan had said she had!

It was too difficult to move on like this. Accepting Nathan and Anna would be like forgetting her own daughter, and she couldn't have that. Not ever.

Free of the crowds, she strode away from the nativity. She couldn't stay there any longer. She couldn't watch the end. All she wanted at that point was to be at home. To be surrounded by the things that made her feel calm again.

Back at her cottage, she threw her keys onto the table by the door and headed straight for the lounge, casting the still wrapped present from Nathan under the tree. She slumped into her favourite couch, settling her gaze upon her pictures of Olivia, on the one on the mantel of her daughter reaching up for those bubbles, which was now surrounded by Christmas holly and mistletoe.

She stared at it for a moment, and then sat forward and spoke out loud. 'She's not you. She could *never* replace you.'

Despite the heartache he was feeling at Sydney's abrupt departure, Nathan gave Anna a huge hug. She'd acted her part in the nativity brilliantly, and it had gone without a hitch. All those people who said you should never work with children or animals were wrong. Bert had done everything Anna had asked of him, and most importantly of all he had kept her safe.

Scooping her up into his arms, Nathan hitched her onto his hip and kissed her cheek. 'Well done, pumpkin.'

'Thanks, Daddy. Did you see me at the end? With my golden halo?'

'I did! Very impressive.'

'I made it in class.'

'It looked very professional.'

'I saw Sydney.'

He frowned, feeling his stomach plummet with dread. What had Anna seen? That Sydney had looked sick? That she'd run?

He'd almost gone after her. One moment she'd been there, and then the next...

'You did? She got called away, I think, towards the end. But she *did* see you, and she was smiling, so she was very proud.'

Anna beamed. 'I'm hungry, Daddy. Can we get something to eat?'

He nodded. 'Sure. I think the hot dog stand may just have a few left if we're quick.'

Putting her back down on the ground, he walked with her over to the fast food stall. He wasn't hungry. Not at all. All he could see was the look on Sydney's face just before she'd turned and bolted.

He'd been too far away to chase after her. Not that he could have done. He'd needed to be here for Anna, just as he'd promised. But he kept replaying in his mind the change that had come over Sydney's features. The brave smile she'd tried to give to his daughter before her face had fallen and she'd gone.

As they passed them various villagers stopped to compliment them and to tell Anna how well she'd done.

'Hey, guess what?' he said, determined to keep things happy and bright for his daughter.

'What?'

'Lottie won the Best Pet competition!'

'She *did*? Yay!' Anna jumped up and down with glee. 'Can we go and get her?'

'Let's eat these first.' He handed her a hot dog, covered with a healthy dollop of fried onions, ketchup and mustard. 'And then we will. Malcolm's looking after the pets at the moment, so she's not on her own.'

Anna bit into her hot dog and wiped her mouth when a piece of fried onion tried to escape. 'Did she get a ribbon?'

'I think she did.'

'And a prize?'

'I think so. She was very lucky, wasn't she?'

He was finding this difficult. Pretending everything was okay when all he wanted to do was sit alone and allow himself to feel miserable. Had he pushed Sydney too hard by giving her that present? Had he tried to make her accept things she wasn't ready to work through yet?

I should never have got involved! I should have kept my distance!

'We had the judge on our side.' Anna smiled and took another bite.

Did we? Maybe only briefly.

He bit into his own hot dog, but he didn't really want it. The smell of the onions only turned his stomach.

She'd not been gone long, but already he ached for her. Missed her. He'd thought for a moment that they had a future together. He'd pictured waking up in the mornings and seeing her next to him. Her grey eyes twinkling at him from her pillow. He'd imagined them taking country walks together, hand in hand, and having picnics in the summer—Sydney laughing in the warm sun, her hair glinting.

He'd imagined nights watching movies together and sharing a bucket of popcorn. Feeding each other tasty morsels and titbits from the fridge before running upstairs, giggling, as he chased her before they fell into bed. And then moments when they'd just talk. He'd hold her hand. Trace the lines on her palm. He'd imagined them making love. Maybe even having a family of their own together...

They could have had it all.

He'd had his heart broken again, and this time he felt even more distraught.

He'd known Gwyneth was selfish. Had always had to have things her own way. She'd always had the perfect life, and a disabled partner had not been for her. Even the promise of a new family, the child they'd made together, hadn't been enough for her. It had never been enough for her. His diagnosis had just been the last thing she'd needed before she walked away. He'd never expected that she would walk away from her own child, too, but she had.

Sydney was looking out for herself too, but in a different way. Her child—Olivia—had been the centre of her life. Her world. And her world had been taken from her. Her sun had been stolen so that she'd only been living in darkness.

Nathan had thought that he'd brightened that darkness for a while.

'Is Sydney coming to our house on Christmas Day?' Anna asked, finishing off her bun in a final mouthful.

'Er… I really don't know, Anna. She's a bit sad at the moment.'

'Because she doesn't have her little girl any more?'

Nathan looked at his daughter, surprised at her insight. 'Yes. I think that's it.'

But what if it wasn't just that?

'We could go to hers and try to cheer her up. It *is* Christmas, and Miss Howarth says it's the season of goodwill. We learnt that at school for the play.'

How simple it was in a child's world. Everything was so black and white. 'We'll see. You might be busy playing with all your new things.'

'Sydney could come and play with me.'

He sighed. 'I don't know, Anna. Perhaps we need to give her some space for a while.'

'I want to thank her for giving Lottie first prize.

Can we go and see her now? Before Christmas Day? Before she gets sad?'

Nathan felt touched by his daughter's compassion. She was doing her best to understand. 'She's already sad. Maybe we'll see her in the village. Come on…let's get Lottie and go home.'

He took her sticky hand in his and together they headed off to the animal tent.

CHAPTER NINE

IT WAS CHRISTMAS MORNING. A day on which Sydney should have been woken by an excited child bouncing on her bed and urging her to go downstairs. Instead, she was woken by the sound of rain against her window, and she lay in bed for a moment, not wanting to move.

Christmas Day.

The house was full of decorations. Encouraged by Nathan, and feeling positive and optimistic, she had adorned the house throughout, sure in the knowledge that this season she would have a reason to celebrate. People she loved to celebrate *with*.

Only it hadn't worked out that way.

She stared at the ceiling and once again asked herself if she was really doing the right thing.

Nathan was a kind-hearted man. Compassionate, caring. And she felt sure he had strong feelings for her. Looking at the pillows beside her, she remembered that night they'd made love. How good he'd made her feel. The brief time that they'd had together had been exquisite. Being made love to, being cherished, being as *treasured* as he had made her feel, had made her realise all that had been missing from her life.

I'm alone.

He'd not come after her after the nativity. He hadn't shown up in the few days afterwards either. She'd thought that he might, and she'd been prepared not to answer the door. To hide. But he hadn't come.

She'd always believed that by keeping her distance from romantic entanglements she was keeping herself safe—and, yes, she supposed she was. But she was also keeping herself in a prison of loneliness. It was a kind of solitary confinement. All she had was Magic, her cat. Her only interactions were with the people and the animals at work and the friendly faces she saw in the shops. When she returned home all she had left were herself and her memories.

Unless I choose Nathan's way of thinking.

Christmas was a time for family. She could be sharing the day with Nathan. With Anna. Darling, sweet little Anna, whom she also adored. And she was letting fear keep her away. Her fear of being vulnerable again. Of losing Nathan. Losing Anna. Of not being enough for either of them!

'I'm losing you if I do nothing!' she said out loud, angry at herself.

Putting on her slippers and grabbing her robe, she headed downstairs.

The Christmas tree twinkled in the corner, with just a few presents underneath it. There was that gift from Nathan. Something from her parents. A couple of gifts from faithful long-term customers at work. The gift she'd placed there in Olivia's memory.

There could have been more. There could have been something for Nathan. For Anna. There could have been happiness in this house again. The day could have been spent the way Christmas is supposed to be spent.

She could be cooking Christmas breakfast for them all right now. Scrambled egg and smoked salmon. Maybe a little Bucks Fizz.

She sat by the tree and picked up the parcel from her mum and dad. It was soft and squidgy, and when she half-heartedly tugged at the wrapping she discovered they'd got her a new pair of fleece pyjamas. She smiled at the pattern—little penguins on tiny icebergs. The other gifts were a bottle of wine, some chocolates, a book…

All that was left was the gift from Nathan and the one for her own daughter that would never be opened.

She picked up the gift from Nathan and glanced at the card.

Merry Christmas, Sydney!
Lots of love, Nathan xxx

What would it be? She had no idea. Part of her felt that it would be wrong to open it now. They weren't together any more. He'd made that clear. She hesitated.

He'd wanted her to have it.

Sydney tore at the wrapping and discovered a plain white box. Frowning, she picked at the tape holding the end closed, getting cross when it wouldn't come free and having to use a pen from her side table to pierce it and break the seal. Inside, something was wrapped in bubble wrap.

She slid it out and slowly unwrapped the plastic. It was a picture frame, and taped to the front, was a small white envelope. There was something inside. A memory card...

It's a digital photo frame.

She plugged it into the mains, inserted the memory card and switched it on, wondering what there could be on it...and gasped.

There, right before her eyes, were pictures of Olivia that she had never even seen before! Some were close-ups, some were group shots, some were of her with other people or children, most she recognised as people from Silverdale.

Olivia in a park on a swing set next to another little boy, who was grinning at the photographer. Olivia at a birthday party with her face all smudged with chocolate cake. Olivia in the front row of the school choir.

She watched in shocked awe as picture after picture of her daughter appeared on the screen.

Where had Nathan got these? They must have come from other people! People in the village who had taken their own photos and captured Olivia in them too. And somehow—amazingly— he had gathered all these pictures together and presented them to her like this!

Tears pricked at her eyes as she gazed at the beautiful images. And then it flicked to another picture, and this one was moving. A video. Of a school play. She remembered it clearly. It had been Olivia's first play and she'd been dressed as a ladybird in a red top that Sydney had spent ages making, sewing on little black dots and then making her a bobble headband for her antennae.

The video showed the last few moments. It captured the applause of the crowd, the kiddies all lining up in a row, taking a bow. A boy near Olivia waved madly at the camera, and then Olivia waved at someone just off to the left of the screen and called out, *'I love you, Mummy!'*

Sydney heard the words and burst into tears, her hands gripping the frame like a lifeline. She'd forgotten that moment. She'd been there. She remembered the play very well; she'd been so proud of Olivia for not forgetting any of her words, and she'd been a true actress, playing her part with aplomb. And at the end she'd seen Sydney in the crowd, and Sydney had waved at her madly and called out to her.

She pressed 'pause'. Then 'rewind'. And watched it again.

Sydney had always believed that she would never get any new photos of Olivia. That her daughter had been frozen in time. But Nathan had given her a gift that she could never have foreseen!

Surely he loved her? What man would do something so thoughtful and as kind as this if he didn't? He would have to know just what this would mean to her.

When the video ended and the frame went back to the beginning of its cycle of photos again, Sydney rushed upstairs to get dressed. She had to see him. She had to...what? Thank him?

'I don't want to thank him. I want to be with him,' she said aloud to Magic, who lay curled on her bed, blinking in irritation at her racing into the bedroom and disturbing her slumber. 'I've been so stupid!'

She yanked off her robe and her pyjamas and kicked off her slippers so hard they flew into the mirror on the wardrobe door.

She pulled on jeans, a tee shirt and a thick fisherman's jumper and twisted her hair up into a rough ponytail. She gave her teeth a quick scrub and splashed her face with some water. Once she'd given it a cursory dry with a towel she raced downstairs and headed for her car, gunning the engine and screeching off down the road.

She hadn't even locked her own front door.

But before she could go to Nathan's house there was somewhere else she needed to go first.

Silverdale Cemetery and Memorial Gardens was a peaceful place. But for a long time it had been somewhere that Sydney had avoided. It had always hurt too much, and for a long time she hadn't come. She'd not felt she had the inner strength to get through a visit.

But today she felt able to be there.

She *wanted* to be.

Today she felt closer to her daughter than on any other day so far. Perhaps it had something to do with what Nathan had said. Perhaps it was because he had helped lift her guilt. Perhaps it was because he had given her that new way of thinking. But now Sydney felt able to go to the site where her daughter was buried, and she knew that she wouldn't stand there staring down at the earth and thinking of her daughter lying there, cold and alone and dead.

Because Olivia wasn't there any more. She wasn't in the ground, cold and dead.

Olivia was alive in her heart. And in her mind. Sydney's head was full of images long since forgotten. Memories were washing over her with the strength of a tsunami, pounding into her with laughter and delight and warm feelings of a life well-lived and enjoyed.

Olivia had been a happy little girl, and Sydney had forgotten that. Focusing too much on her last day. The day on which she'd been dying. Unconscious. Helpless. In pain.

Now Sydney had a new outlook on her daughter's life. And it was an outlook she knew Olivia would approve of. So the cemetery was no longer a place for her to fear but a place in which she could go and sit quietly for a moment, after laying some flowers. Bright, colourful winter blooms that her daughter had helped her to plant years before.

The headstone was a little dirty, so she cleaned it off with her coat sleeve and made sure her daughter's name was clear and bright. Her eyes closed as she pictured her daughter watering the flowers in the back garden with her pink tin watering can.

'I'm sorry I haven't visited for a while,' she said, her eyes still closed. 'But I got caught up in feeling sorry for myself. You wouldn't have approved.' She laughed slightly and smiled, feeling tears prick at her eyes. 'But I think I'm overcoming that. A new friend—a *good* friend—taught me a valuable lesson. I was stuck, you see, Olivia. Stuck on missing you. Stuck on taking the blame because I felt someone had to.'

She opened her eyes and smiled down at the ground and the headstone.

'I don't have to do that any more. I'm not stuck. I'm free. And because I'm free you are too. I can see you now. In my head. In here...' She tapped her chest, over her heart. 'I can see you so clearly! I can hear you and smell you and feel you in my arms.'

She paused, gathering her breath.

'You'd like Nathan. He's a doctor. He's a good man. And Anna...his daughter...you'd love her too. I know you would. I guess I just wanted to say that I...I *love* you, Olivia. I'm sorry I was gone for a while, but I'm back, and now I have someone looking out for me, and he's given me the ability to get *you* back the way I should have from the beginning.'

She touched the headstone.

'I'll be back more often from now on. And… er…I've put up a tree. I'm celebrating Christmas this year. There's something for you under it. You won't ever be forgotten.'

She sniffed in the cold, crisp December air and looked about her. Two headstones away was the grave of one Alfred Courtauld, and she remembered his wife telling her about how she'd once laid a flower on Olivia's grave.

Sydney picked up a flower from Olivia's bouquet and laid it on Alfred's stone. 'Thanks for looking after Olivia whilst I've been away.'

And then she slowly walked back to her car.

Nathan watched as Anna unwrapped her brand-new bike, her hands ripping off the swathes of reindeer-patterned paper that he'd wrapped it in, smiling warmly at her cries of joy and surprise.

'A *bike!*' she squealed, swinging her leg over the frame and getting onto the seat. 'Can I ride it? Can I take it outside?'

'Course you can.' He helped her take the bike out to the back garden and watched as she eagerly began to pedal, wobbling alarmingly at the beginning, but then soon getting the hang of it.

'Look, Daddy!'

'I'm watching, baby.'

He stood in the doorway, holding his mug of coffee, watching his daughter cycle up and down, but feeling sad that he couldn't give her more. He'd hoped this Christmas to be sharing the day with Sydney. To be opening presents together, giving Anna the feel of a *real* family, so the three of them could enjoy the day together because they were meant to be together.

But Sydney had kept her distance. She'd not dumped him as unceremoniously as Gwyneth had, but she'd still broken his heart.

It wasn't just Christmas he felt sad about. It was all of it. Every day. Christmas was a time for family, but so was the rest of the year. Waking every morning *together*. Listening to each other talk about their day each evening. Laughing. *Living*.

He'd hoped that Sydney could be in their lives, and he knew that Anna still hoped for that, too.

She'd kept going on about it last night before she went to bed.

'Will Sydney be coming tomorrow, Daddy?'

But, sadly, the answer had been no. She would not be coming.

As he headed into the kitchen to make himself a fresh drink he briefly wondered if she had opened his present. It had taken a lot of organising, but Mrs Courtauld had helped—reaching out to people, contacting them on her walks around the village with her greyhound Prince, asking everyone to check their photos and see if any of them had Olivia in them.

He'd dared to hope there would be one or two, but he had been surprised at how many they had got. Fourteen new pictures of Olivia and a video, in which she was saying the exact words he knew would gladden Sydney's heart.

Because that was what he wanted for her most of all. For her to be happy. For her heart to swell once again with love. He'd hoped that her love would include him, but…

His doorbell buzzed. *Who on earth…?*

It was Christmas morning. It couldn't be a door-to-door salesman, or anyone like that. Perhaps someone had been taken ill? Perhaps he was needed as a doctor?

He hurried to the front door, unlocked it and swung it open.

'Sydney?'

She looked out of breath, edgy and anxious. 'Can I come in?'

Did he want her to? Of course he did! He'd missed her terribly. But if she was just here to re-hash everything they'd said the other night then he wasn't sure he wanted to hear it.

But something in her eyes—a brightness, a *hope*—made him give her one last audience.

He stepped back. 'Please.'

He watched as she brushed past and then followed her into the kitchen, from where she could see Anna, playing happily in the back garden.

'You got her a bike?'

He smiled as he looked at his daughter, happily pedalling away. 'Yes. It was what she wanted.'

Sydney turned to him. 'And what do *you* want, Nathan? For Christmas?'

Nathan stared at her, trying to gauge the exact reason for her turning up like this on Christmas

Day. It wouldn't be a trick or a game. Sydney wasn't like that. *Had she opened his gift to her?*

He couldn't answer her. Couldn't tell her what he *really* wanted. So he changed the subject. 'Did you like your present?'

Tears filled her eyes then and she nodded, the movement of her head causing the tears to run freely down her cheeks. She wiped them away hurriedly. 'I can't believe what you did. How you managed that... I'm...speechless.'

He gave a small smile. 'I wanted to make you happy. Just tell me it didn't make you sad.'

'It didn't.' She took a quick step towards him, then stopped. 'I've come to apologise. I made a mistake.'

Nathan frowned. 'What do you mean?'

'Us. I made the wrong choice.'

He didn't say anything. He didn't want to make this go wrong. He needed to hear what she had to say.

'I got frightened. The day...the evening we were together I...panicked. And then, when I saw Anna on the donkey, I don't know what it was...I started feeling guilty. I felt that if I forgot Olivia on her most important day I would be losing her. But then today—earlier—I realised that it *wasn't* her most important day. The day she died. Her most important day was the day she was born! I can remember Olivia in a different way, just like you said, and by doing so I can also have a future. And so can she. Because my grief was trapping Olivia too. I kept her in pain all that time. Remembering the day she left me...when she was suffering. When I couldn't help her. I kept her there. Trapped in time. But not any more. Not any more,' she said firmly.

He shook his head. 'Love isn't what hurts people, Sydney. *Losing* someone hurts. *Grief* hurts. *Pain* hurts. But love? Love is the greatest thing we can experience.'

'I know. Because I feel love for Olivia. I feel love for...' She paused and stepped closer, laying a hand upon his chest, over his heart. 'For you. I've felt more helpless in the last few days being sat alone at home than I have ever felt. I need to be with you.'

He laid his hand over hers, feeling his heart pound in his ribcage as if it was a wild animal, trying desperately to escape. 'What are you saying?'

'I'm saying I want us to be together. You. Me. Anna. I think we can do it. I think that together we can be strong enough to fight whatever is coming in the future.'

'You mean it?' he asked, hope in his voice.

'I do. I've missed you so much! I've been in pain because I don't have you. I didn't realise what was missing from my life until I met you.'

Nathan smiled and kissed her, meeting her lips with a kiss that burned with fervour. Devouring her, tasting her, enjoying her with a passion that he could barely contain.

She wanted him! She wanted him back and she was willing to take a chance on their future.

It was all he'd ever wanted.

None of them knew what his future would be. How his disease would progress. Whether it would get worse. Just because that happened to a lot of people with MS, it didn't mean it would happen to him. He might be one of the lucky ones. It could stay as relapsing remitting. Who knew?

And even if it did progress he now felt braver about facing it. Because he would have Sydney at his side. And Anna, too. His daughter would not be burdened by carrying the weight of her father's illness all alone on her young shoulders. She would be able to share her worries. With a mother figure. With *Sydney*. And he knew Anna adored Sydney. They could be a perfect family. Or at least they could try!

They broke apart at the sound of his daughter's footsteps running towards the house.

'Sydney!' Anna barrelled into them both, enveloping them with her arms. 'Are you here for Christmas dinner?'

Sydney smiled at Nathan, and he answered. 'She's here for *every* dinner, I think. Aren't you?'

He looked into her grey eyes and saw happiness there. And joy.

'If you'll have me.'

Anna squeezed her tight and beamed.

Nathan pulled her close, so they were both wrapped in his embrace.

'Always.'

* * * * *

If you enjoyed this story, check out these other great reads from Louisa Heaton

SEVEN NIGHTS WITH HER EX
ONE LIFE-CHANGING NIGHT
A FATHER THIS CHRISTMAS?
HIS PERFECT BRIDE

All available now!